The Cauldron's Gift

MARINA FINLAYSON

FINESSE SOLUTIONS

Cover design by Karri Klawiter
Editing by Larks & Katydids
Formatting by Polgarus Studio

Published by Finesse Solutions Pty Ltd
2016/6/#01

Author's note: This book was written and produced in Australia and
uses British/Australian spelling conventions, such as "colour" instead
of "color", and "-ise" endings instead of "-ize" on words like "realise".

National Library of Australia Cataloguing-in-Publication entry:

Finlayson, Marina, author.
The cauldron's gift / Marina Finlayson.
ISBN 9780994239150 (paperback)
Finlayson, Marina. Magic's return; bk. 2.
Fantasy fiction.
A823.4

*For Brian Caswell. Thank you for not laughing
at my thirteen-year-old efforts.*

Chapter One

Plenty of teenagers don't share a house with their dad, but usually it's because their parents are divorced. Not because he's a bear.

"Crystal!" Mum stood at the foot of the stairs, jiggling her car keys, her green eyes snapping with impatience. "Hurry up. You don't want to keep your father waiting, do you?"

"Seriously, Mum?" CJ appeared in the bathroom doorway, arms folded across her pyjama-clad chest, and glared down at Mum. Oh, no. I'd seen that look before. In fact, Mum was wearing a nearly identical one. They were way too much alike. Both tall, dark, and beautiful—and stubborn as they came. "You really think he's hanging out for our visit?"

"Absolutely. You're not even dressed yet. What have you been doing in there all this time?"

"I'm not coming. What's the point? He doesn't even know who we are."

"Of course he does. How can you say that?"

"Because it's true, Mum! Wake up and smell the roses." She went back into the bathroom and slammed the door.

Mum's face went red. Either she was about to cry, or CJ was going to cop an earful. My money was on the earful.

"Crystal Jane! Get down here right now!"

"Mum." I grabbed at her arm before she'd gone more than two steps up the stairs. Even for CJ, there was a lot more door-slamming going on around here lately than usual. "Let's just go without her this time, okay?"

You could hardly blame her for being upset. We all were. Mum was always tired and snappy these days, lines of worry permanently engraved into her forehead. CJ was a door-slamming, screeching harpy, and I—I was just trying to keep the peace between them. Dad had always been good at that, with his stupid dad jokes and his knack for always lightening the mood—but of course, Dad wasn't here any more, and that was the whole problem. It turned out that my easygoing, slightly daggy dad had been the glue holding our little family of four together.

Mum backed the car out of the garage, her lips pressed tightly together, holding in all the things she wanted to say but thought she shouldn't. One day she was going to crack, and it would be like when Pandora opened the box and all the nasties flew out, spreading their evil across the world. There'd be only one shrivelled little piece of Mum left over, fluttering hopelessly inside still trying to escape.

We'd been driving for ten minutes before she trusted herself to speak. It was funny, really. Dad and I were the redheads of the family, but Mum and CJ had the tempers.

"She should have come. I should have made her."

Right. Like anyone could make CJ do anything she didn't want to do. Mum had certainly never been able to, and it hadn't gotten any easier since Dad's … incident. CJ hardly even listened to me, and I was her twin. Her shorter, far less glamorous, twin. Sadly, we weren't identical.

"I think she's got a lot of maths homework," I said.

"And you don't?"

"We're not in the same class this year," I reminded her, though of course I did have maths homework, along with an Ancient History essay due Monday and a Chemistry prac to write up. Even if, by some miracle, we hadn't had any homework, Year 12 was our final year of school, and we were expected to spend our free time studying. The teachers made it sound like our final exams in the Higher School Certificate would define the whole course of our lives, instead of just deciding which university courses we could get into. Sure, they were important. I got that. But some of us had a few other crises going on right now, and those exams were still months away.

Currently our family was caught up in the middle of the biggest magical attack since the so-called fraud of the Cottingley fairy photos of the 1920s. There was a hole somehow in the prison walls the warders had set up two centuries before to keep the Sidhe and their mischief out of our world, a hole that no one had been able to find yet, let alone plug. Dad had been a bear for nearly five months now because of it, and our little family hadn't been coping too well with the new reality. Compared to that, the HSC would be a walk in the park. It was hard to get too excited about distant exams when at any moment the Sidhe could break free and turn the world on its head.

More than they had already, that is.

It had all started in September last year, when a beautiful girl was found comatose in a glass coffin in a clearing in the forest, in a horrible parody of Snow White. CJ and I had been next hit, with our own version of the Toads and Diamonds fairy tale. I liked frogs as much as the next person, but having one jump out of your mouth every time you opened it got old *real* fast. Nothing more had happened in the months since Dad had been cursed with his own fairytale nightmare, but that didn't mean anyone among the warders had relaxed, even if we no longer made front page news.

"How's he been this week?"

The car sped down the Gore Hill Freeway, Sydney's now-familiar silhouette rearing against the sky up ahead. Lanes merged and diverged, funnelling cars toward the centre of the city. Even on a Saturday morning there was plenty of traffic.

"Oh, you know. Much the same."

"Has he been using his words?"

Mum paused. Because she was concentrating on changing lanes, or because she didn't want to answer? That had been the other big surprise of the fairytale attacks—learning that our own parents were part of a secret Council dedicated to keeping the Sidhe, a race of magical beings, locked in a magical prison so they couldn't harm humans any more.

Fairy tales: not just for children, as it turned out.

Mum was a warder, same as Dad, and very tight-lipped about anything to do with magic. They'd been keeping secrets so long it was second nature to her now.

"No," she said at last.

I looked out the window. That was bad news. It kind of took the shine off the view, which usually managed to cheer me up.

We were on the deck of the Sydney Harbour Bridge, and Sydney spread out before us like a postcard. It was a picture-perfect day: the harbour sparkled in the hot February sun, and the Opera House flung its graceful white sails against a clear blue summer sky. The city was showing the world its prettiest face. A great day to be a tourist.

Not so good if you were a polar bear.

Not that there ever was a good time to be a polar bear when you were supposed to be a man, but Dad had really been feeling the heat lately. They'd installed a small pool for him last month, and he spent a lot of time lolling in the water, the hair on his big shaggy head all spiky with damp.

Headquarters was in the heart of The Rocks, just a hop, skip, and a jump from the bridge's exit ramp. Mum cut through narrow back streets and we were soon pulling into the underground parking garage of a long, low, red-brick building, its arched upper windows looking out across the harbour.

We took the lift to the ground floor, but Mum stopped me with a hand on my arm as the doors opened.

"Do you want me to come in with you?"

"No, it's fine. You've got your work. I'll come upstairs and find you a bit later."

"Okay." Still she didn't let go of my arm. "Don't forget, don't go in if he's asleep."

She'd told me that almost every visit. "He's not a wild animal, Mum—it's Dad. He's not going to leap up and tear my head off if I startle him."

She gave me a tired excuse for a smile. "I'm just saying—be careful."

I stepped out of the lift and left her standing there, an anxious look in her eye. Poor Mum. The biggest crisis in warding history, and her workload had suddenly doubled. There were supposed to be seven warders, but one had been turned into an ogre in the fairytale attacks. No one had quite figured out which fairy tale that was from—there were plenty that featured ogres. Dad was also a warder, and he was out of action too, which left Mum and the other four warders putting in long hours.

In spite of all their knowledge, the warders were hampered by the fact that magic was no longer possible for them. Human mages had shaped the prison that trapped the Sidhe long ago, but, ironically enough, their act meant that humans couldn't work magic any more. Aether, the raw material of magic, was all trapped inside the Sidhe prison too, except for a little stored in special vaults in our world. Without it, the warders were reduced to magicology, which was a kind of hybrid child of magic and science. It used their tiny stores of aether and whatever their human ingenuity could invent, and was a gadget-lover's dream. They had machines that could measure the presence of aether or capture it—they even had apps. Magic had come into the twenty-first century, but the lack of aether severely hampered what the warders could do.

Despite their work, no one had yet been able to find a way to reverse either spell. Dad himself was the best magicologist they had, which made things tricky when he was the one targeted. It had been Dad who'd made the breakthrough that had helped CJ and me cope when we'd been hit with the delightful toads and diamonds curse last year. Every time CJ spoke she'd dripped diamonds, and I'd been the lucky one cursed to spit frogs and toads with every word. Within days Dad had rigged a way to dampen the effects of the spell. I'd never understood how, but I hadn't cared, as long as it worked.

I'd never thought Dad would still be trapped in his own fairytale nightmare nearly five months later.

Dad was housed in what had once been a large meeting room at the back of the building. There was a smaller room between it and the corridor, not much more than a cubbyhole really. When I opened the door it bumped the chair of the young guy working on his laptop there.

"Hi, Simon."

Simon was one of my favourite seekers. Despite the fact that our friendship had gotten off to a pretty shaky start, I'd eventually realised he did have a heart hidden somewhere under that rather grouchy exterior. He'd proved it when his kiss of true love had woken our poor sleeping Snow White.

"Hey, Vi," he said. "Come to see your dad?"

Guarding a polar bear probably wasn't what he'd signed up for when he became a seeker, but it couldn't all be glamorous assignments roaming the world looking for magical artefacts. Someone always had to do the crappy jobs.

"Yeah. How is he today?" I peeked through the small glass pane set into the inner door, but couldn't see Dad in the dim light inside.

"Seems tired." Simon stood up and looked through the window, too. He was much taller than me and had to stoop to do so. "He's awake now, though."

I nodded and tried the handle, but it wouldn't move.

"You're locking this now?" It wasn't as if Dad, with his bear claws, could open the door anyway, but they shouldn't lock him in. He wasn't a prisoner. "Who ordered that?"

Probably Dorian. I liked him the least of the warders. The seven of them were supposed to be equals, but he acted like he was the boss a little too often for my taste.

Simon produced a key and unlocked it for me.

"Your mother," he said, and closed the door behind me when I stepped through.

Mum? Why would she give an order like that? I moved further into the room and saw Dad stretched out on the floor along the far wall, doing his best impression of a bearskin rug. The blinds were drawn on the high windows above him, to keep out the heat. They only looked out on the lane that ran behind the building anyway, so he wasn't missing out on much of a view.

"Hey, Dad," I said. "It's me."

He raised his massive head and blinked at me.

"How are you? Want me to read to you?"

He yawned, showing those massive teeth. I went to him and dropped to my knees beside him. His head was huge, easily three times as big as my own. I circled his neck with my arms and leaned in for a hug, his coarse hair tickling my face. He huffed hot breath against my ear. He smelled of fish and damp fur.

"Been swimming today?"

He made a noise halfway between a groan and another yawn, and let his great head sink back onto his front paws. Maybe he was tired, as Simon had said, but usually I got a lot more reaction than this. Last week I'd read to him, one of his favourite Tom Clancy novels, but when I went to the shelves it wasn't there. None of his books were.

I stuck my head out the door and Simon looked up enquiringly.

"What happened to Dad's books?"

"He shredded them."

"What, all of them?"

He shrugged. "The ones he didn't shred he chucked in the pool. Either way, they're ruined."

"Okaaay."

I closed the door and turned back to Dad. He hadn't moved, hardly even seemed to be aware that I was still here. The room was cool, but he was panting. Poor thing. Fur coats and the Australian summer just didn't go together.

I grabbed the big roll of plastic that had all Dad's words printed on it, and unrolled it on the floor by his head.

"Dad? You hungry? Want something to eat?"

The plastic was covered in words, symbols, pictures. It showed the marks of his sharp claws, where he'd pointed to fish, or ice, or various members of staff. At first the other warders had hoped to access Dad's scientific knowledge, but we'd soon learned that wasn't possible. His ability to communicate was limited by the bear form he inhabited; he could no longer form complex thoughts or deal in abstract ideas, but we'd managed "conversation" of sorts. Enough to know there was truly a man inside the bear skin.

He grunted, and heaved himself to his feet so suddenly I had to scramble to get out of his way. Ignoring the words, he trampled across the sheet of plastic, leaving a few more dints and scratches in its surface, and slid into his pool. Water sloshed over the low side as his great bulk displaced it, spilling across the floor.

I sat on the edge of the pool and watched him rolling around. The water wasn't deep enough to let him swim. I'd seen footage of polar bears swimming; despite the layers of fat they looked almost graceful as their dinner-plate-sized feet churned through the water. Dad sprawled like a drunk, his dirty-white stomach rising like a mini-iceberg from the water.

"CJ sends her love," I said when he'd stopped splashing. My pants were wet, but it didn't matter. I had plenty of clothes here; the place was like a second home now. "We're going shopping later to buy a present for Sona—you remember her, don't you? She was the one I told you about, that was in the cathedral with me and Zac when the Morrigan attacked. She was very brave. It's her eighteenth birthday party next weekend."

I kept chatting, filling him in on all the news I could think of. His eyelids sagged closed, so I couldn't tell if he was listening or not, but I couldn't blame him if he found it boring. That life, with school and friends and home, seemed so irrelevant in this room. I stared at the enormous bear and let my words peter out.

My dad was a polar bear. Except for the fact that I'd sat so close to him for the last half-hour without injury, there was nothing to show he was my dad at all. Had he even looked at me? I felt the prick of hopeless tears and scrubbed them away angrily. What was the point of sitting here telling all this stuff to a dumb animal? What was I hoping for? That he'd suddenly start chatting away, telling me one of his stupid jokes? CJ was right. Coming here was a waste of time.

Might as well say goodbye. I leaned over and rested a hand on his head. He jerked awake with a snarl, and one paw came out of the water with frightening speed. I leapt up, but the tip of a sharp claw raked the side of my face.

I screamed and the door behind me burst open.

"Violet! What's wrong?"

I backed away, but the bear showed no more interest in me. He grunted and settled back into the water. I pressed my hand to my cheek, feeling the warmth of blood dripping between my fingers.

Simon grabbed me and pulled me quickly from the room. "Let me see that. What happened?"

"It's nothing," I said. "Just a scratch."

My hand shook as he pulled it gently away and inspected the wound. That was my *dad*. And he'd just attacked me.

Simon met my eyes. "He's not himself lately."

No, he wasn't. He was a bear, and growing more bear-like every day. Hot tears stung my eyes. If we didn't find a cure for him soon, Dad might be lost forever.

Chapter Two

Simon wanted to bandage my face, but I wasn't having any of that. Wouldn't I look gorgeous walking around with a line of Band-Aids on my face, like some teenage guy who'd managed to slice himself open shaving? No, thanks. Once it stopped bleeding, it wasn't really much of a wound. I let him swipe me with antiseptic, but that was as much fussing as I could handle. I just wanted to get away from the sympathy in Simon's eyes.

I'd told Mum I'd catch up with her when I was finished with Dad, but now there would be questions, and awkward explanations. Not to mention I-told-you-sos: *Didn't I tell you not to touch him if he was asleep? Didn't I tell you that?* But it was *Dad*. It shouldn't matter. He loved us. Awake or asleep, he would never do anything to hurt us.

Out in the hall again, I leaned against the wall and touched the cut, probing gently with my fingers. It stung, like someone had laid a line of hot wax down my cheek. My eyes stung too, and I let out a shaky breath. I was too old for tears. I fumbled my phone out of my pocket and dialled a familiar number.

Zac picked up on the third ring.

"Hey, there." His voice held a special warmth that was only for me. "How's my favourite girl?"

"Not so hot, actually." My voice quivered, and I cleared my throat, horrified. I was *not* going to cry. "I've just been in to see Dad, and he—he—"

"He what?"

Tears threatened. I waited until I could say it without breaking down. It helped to know that Zac was on the other end. No one else cared about me the way he did.

"He attacked me. I'm okay," I added hurriedly as he drew in a shocked breath. "Just a bit … upset. It was just a scratch, but …"

"I hate this." His voice was tight with suppressed anger. "This whole stupid mess with the Sidhe. It's so unfair. I wish there was something I could do, but there's not, and I hate that, too. I feel so useless."

"It helps just to have someone to talk to about it." He sounded really uptight. He was usually much more laid back. "Do you want to come over tonight and watch a movie or something?"

"Sorry, I can't. Got a family thing on."

Damn. Well, it wasn't as if he could actually do anything to help. I knew what he meant about feeling useless. It didn't seem like there was anything anyone could do, and sitting around waiting for the next disaster to strike was making me crazy. But it did make me feel better to look into his warm brown eyes and see how much he cared. And hey—at least his family life was normal. Sometimes when I was at his house I could forget all about magic and fairies and their stupid, stupid curses.

"Okay. Maybe tomorrow, then. I'll call you."

On impulse I took the lift down to the basement, looking for Gretel or Ronnie, my two best friends in the organisation. They'd helped me save CJ from the Morrigan last year. They were twins, too—there were a lot of twins among the warders, they ran in magical families—though they were identical. They were still easy to tell apart, though, since Ronnie's hair was cut close to her scalp, and Gretel's fell in long waves down her back.

I looked inside Ronnie's usual lab, but she wasn't there. Nor was she in the server room, checking on the computers. Coming out of the server room, I nearly walked straight into Dorian, my favourite warder. Not.

He recoiled in shock, brandishing a wicked-looking knife. I stepped hurriedly out of range.

"Watch where you're going!" he snapped.

"What are you doing, waving that around?"

I knew I sounded cross, but he'd scared the crap out of me. There was a faint whiff of burnt toffee in the air too, which set my nerves jangling. That was the smell of aether, the raw material of magic. I dragged my eyes away from the knife, expecting to see his usual supercilious look, but his face was deathly pale, with huge shadows under his eyes like bruises. What the hell was wrong with him? I'd seen him only last weekend, and he looked like he'd aged ten years in a week.

For a moment I was worried he was going to use the knife on himself; he looked that bad, as if his whole world had collapsed since the last time I'd seen him. Had something gone terribly wrong that I didn't know about? Any more wrong than having two of the seven warders trapped in fairytale curses, that is.

"I'm returning it to the vault. Not that it's any of your business."

He stalked off, and I watched him turn down the side corridor that led to the vault, which housed our supply of aether, ringed around with iron as well as more mundane protections. The vault was also home to all the magical artefacts that the seekers had gathered in their forays around the world. Even though there wasn't enough aether in the world to power them any more, the warders didn't like having such things out in the general populace. Just in case.

I hesitated. What was Dorian doing, wandering around with a knife in his hand? And a knife that had some kind of magical connection, presumably, if it had come from the vault and carried the scent of aether with it.

He was right; it was none of my business, and soon Mum would be wondering where I'd got to. I should go back upstairs. And I didn't even like Dorian. But curiosity got the better of me in the end. If I was Superman, curiosity was my kryptonite. It was just lucky I wasn't a cat or there'd have been trouble.

I headed down the side corridor after Dorian, stopping along the way to poke my head into various rooms. I *was* still looking for Gretel, after all. Checking up on a warder had nothing to do with it.

A few moments later Dorian passed me again, heading back towards the lifts, and I gave up exploring side rooms and marched straight to the double doors that led through to the vault.

Inside was a large room full of computers and wall panels covered with lights and dials. A couple of smaller rooms opened off it, including the main vault itself. I'd never been in there.

A dark-haired woman looked up from her computer and smiled as I came in. It was Kerrie, one of the seekers. Her brother Bryan was a warder. We'd called her Snow White at first, CJ and I, when we'd seen her on TV. She'd been the first to be hit by a fairytale curse, found lying in a glass coffin in a clearing in the Blue Mountains, unable to be woken. We'd never dreamed then that soon we'd meet her, and discover the magical heritage of our own family. I'd even helped to wake her from her enchanted sleep, though no one knew that but Simon. It had been my idea for him to kiss her. They said that true love's kiss was the antidote to many a spell.

She was pretty, a few years older than me, with long black hair and the kind of full pink lips that looked like they'd been made for kissing. She'd made a lovely Snow White. No wonder Simon had wanted to kiss her.

"Hi," she said. "What's up?"

"Nothing. You seen Gretel?"

"She's in there." She jerked her head at the massive steel door to the vault. "Just putting something away for Warder Kincumber. What happened to your face?"

I shrugged. "It's just a scratch."

If she had been Gretel, or Ronnie, I might have told her, but I didn't know Kerrie well enough. I'd only seen her a few times since she'd woken up. She usually worked out of the Perth branch, and wasn't in Sydney very often.

Which was a shame, since I'd been kind of hoping Simon's

major-league crush might be rewarded with a romance. They were both in their mid-twenties and would have made a good-looking couple, but since he was stationed in Sydney there was nothing doing. For all I knew, she had a boyfriend tucked away in Perth.

The massive steel door behind her swung open and Gretel came through. I caught a glimpse of the artefacts arrayed on their shelves before the door closed again: musical instruments, drinking horns, mirrors and combs, pots, jugs, and containers of many kinds. Artefacts rarely looked like anything special.

Gretel smiled, though there were tired rings under her eyes. "Hello, Vi. Had a good week?"

"Yeah. Okay." I didn't want to tell her about Dad in front of Kerrie. "Has something else happened? I just saw Dorian and he looked terrible."

The two women exchanged glances.

"I think Warder Kincumber has some troubles at home," Gretel said. "And none of us are getting much sleep."

"Was that knife an artefact? I didn't know we had any weapons."

"We keep them separate from the other artefacts."

"But what was he doing with it? I thought none of the artefacts worked with all the aether gone?" Though that one had sure smelled like it was still charged with aether.

"Some of them still retain a little of their own. Enough for a small ritual," Gretel said, which didn't exactly answer the question. Even Gretel suffered from the warders' pathological fear of giving away information.

What kind of ritual used magic knives? I'd heard that there

was blood involved in the original spell, the one that had sucked all the aether in the world here to Australia and anchored it, collapsing all the entries to the Sidhe world. Warder blood, though no one had ever got specific about it, and I still had some uncomfortable questions about the process.

Maybe Dorian was looking so sick from blood loss, if the warders had to keep doing some bloody ritual to keep the seals on the Sidhe prison holding. Though I had trouble imagining my elegant mother doing anything quite so earthy as a blood ritual.

"Can I see them? The weapons?"

Gretel shook her head. "Access is strictly limited. I'm afraid you don't have the security clearance for it."

Well, that figured. The warders had done nothing but make me feel like an inconvenience ever since I'd arrived. A child to be patted on the head and told to sit quietly in the corner. And hey, maybe I'd be happy to do that if I thought they had everything under control. But here we were, five months later, and Dad was still a bear. There was a traitor in the ranks, and they were no closer to finding out who it was. If the warders were so capable, why hadn't they made any progress?

In the morning, CJ was up before me, despite being out late at the movies. I'd heard her come in before I went to sleep, and expected her to lie in bed most of the morning, but there she was, fully dressed and looking remarkably alert for someone who claimed to be unable to function without ten hours of sleep.

"What happened to your face?" she asked when I came down

for breakfast. She was curled up on the lounge with the Sunday paper, supposedly keeping up with world events for her Legal Studies class, but more likely reading the society and entertainment pages.

I was getting mighty tired of answering that question. The conversation with Mum had not gone well. "Dad scratched it."

"You mean the bear attacked you?" That got her to put the paper down.

I gritted my teeth. He was Dad, not *the bear*. "No, he didn't *attack* me. It was just a … a misunderstanding."

"You're as bad as Mum. What are you going to do now? Keep on going until he eats you?"

"Oh, for God's sake, Crystal." I only ever called her Crystal when I was seriously annoyed with her. "He's not going to eat me. It's Dad."

"It's a bear," she corrected. "Dad's gone, and we're not going to get him back unless we do something. Those idiots down at headquarters couldn't find their arses with both hands. They haven't even figured out yet who switched the cauldron, and you wouldn't think that would be too challenging. There aren't that many suspects."

"Oh, so you know how to break a Sidhe curse, do you? Please share, I'm sure everyone would love to know."

"No need to get all snooty about it. But they obviously don't have a clue what they're doing. How long are we going to wait while they fart around? By the time they get something figured out, Dad will be so used to being a bear he'll still want raw fish for breakfast and he won't be able to do anything except lie around in a toddler pool all day."

I poured milk onto my cereal and sat at the round breakfast table. I often sat here alone these days. It used to be the four of us would have breakfast together on Sundays. Dad's specialty was bacon and eggs, and sometimes Mum would cook omelettes. I didn't think she'd even come home last night. She'd been sleeping at work a lot lately.

"Well, I'd love to be able to do something but, frankly, I don't have a clue what to do either, so …" And Dad wasn't *gone*. He still had plenty of lucid days. Yesterday was just a glitch.

"Yeah, but they keep doing the same things. That's the definition of madness, isn't it? Keep doing the same thing but expecting a different outcome? It's pretty obvious by now that their stupid magicology isn't going to work."

"But what else can they do? It's not like modern medicine is equipped to turn bears back into people."

"They could try magic."

I laid my spoon down and stared at her. She had such a superior look on her face I wanted to punch her, but it was really too early and I hadn't slept well.

"Okay. One, that is just crazy, and two—even if they wanted to, how are they going to do magic when we don't have enough aether to work it?"

"What about all that aether in the vault? They could use that."

"That's only enough to power the Hendrix counters and their other little gadgets." And then I stopped, thinking of what else was in the vault.

"What?" CJ's twin spidey-sense was immediately alert.

"Gretel told me yesterday that some of the artefacts in the vault still have some aether."

"You mean they still work? Which ones?"

"You think she'd tell me something like that? You know what they're like!" In some ways I couldn't blame them. Everyone knew there was a traitor, but no one knew who it was, which made everybody jumpy and untrusting. "I've got no idea what they've got tucked away in there. The one I saw yesterday was a knife. Dorian had been using it for something."

"I bet they've got something in there that could help Dad, if they only had the guts to use it."

"They're trying to keep magic out, not use it." I felt compelled to defend the warders, even though I more than half agreed with CJ. But my brushes with the power of magic had left me a little warier than she was. "Who knows what that might do to the seals?"

"Nobody. But that's the point. They're too scared to try anything out of the box. They've been hoarding every last scrap of aether, keeping all their magic secrets, guarding their precious four treasures, for the last two centuries. They can't bear to think of actually *using* any of it."

"Three treasures now."

That was kind of our fault, too. Not that anybody else had been doing a better job of protecting the cauldron. It should have been safe in the Louvre in Paris, not masquerading as an ancient Spartan jug in an exhibition at the Art Gallery here in Sydney. And we'd done our best—four teenagers against the Morrigan, ancient Celtic goddess of war. Not exactly a fair fight. But with a little help from Gretel, Ronnie, and Kerrie we'd managed to send the Morrigan back to her prison. It was just unfortunate that the fabled cauldron of the Dagda went along for the ride as well.

"Three, then." She waved her hand impatiently. "Why don't they try using them, instead of hiding them away? They're not doing anyone any good as they are."

"Use them for what, exactly?" My cereal was getting soggy. I didn't feel like eating anyway. "Two of them are weapons." I'd never seen them, but I knew of the sword of Nuada and the spear of Lugh. Not exactly suited to modern warfare. "The other one is a stone that cries out when the rightful king of Ireland steps on it. Fat lot of good that's going to be."

"True." She got a thoughtful look on her face. Uh-oh. I knew that look. How many times had I ended up in trouble because of that look? Like the time when we were little and she convinced me to water Mum's plants with bleach. To clean them, she said. Or the time she dyed my orange curls black to match her own sleek hair and then tried to straighten it with the iron. It had taken years for my hair to grow back to its original length. "Shame it was the cauldron we lost. It seems to be the most useful of the four. We could have pulled anything out of that sucker. I bet it would have given us a cure for Dad."

"Maybe." It was supposed to be able to provide whatever the user wished for. It had certainly worked a treat when I'd needed weapons to use against the Morrigan. But miracle cures? Who knew? "Doesn't really make any difference, though, does it, since it's in fairyland and we're not."

"Hmmm." That *hmmm* sounded suspicious, but all she said was: "We should do some research. There must be a way to use the others for something."

"Someone would have thought of it by now if there was."

"No, they wouldn't. Haven't you been listening? They're all

running scared, too afraid to think outside the box. And maybe we can find a list of all the artefacts they're hoarding, and what they can do." Her eyes drifted to the livid red line down my face. "I don't think Dad's got much time left."

"Fine." I was scared, too. Yesterday that bear had seemed nothing but a bear. I got up and binned the rest of my cereal. "We'll look in the library."

"In the restricted section."

"In the restricted section, then, if you insist." It was kept locked, but when had a little detail like that ever bothered CJ? "When do you want to start?"

"Mum wants us to meet her in town for dinner. We could go in early, check out the markets, then have a look."

I blinked. Dad's fate was in our hands, but apparently we had time to go shopping first. "The markets in The Rocks?"

They were just down the road from headquarters. It was there the Morrigan had given me that damned origami bird, back when she was still pretending to be my Ancient History teacher. You could never trust a fairy gift, and I'd known that, but I'd been no match for the Morrigan's mental compulsions. Somehow I'd found myself accepting the gift and then forgetting I even had it.

"Yeah. I said I'd meet someone there this afternoon."

"Who? Not Ashleigh?" CJ's best friend didn't like me any more than I liked her. An afternoon in her company wouldn't do anything to improve my mood. Maybe I could talk Zac into coming, despite his allergy to shopping. That would help.

"No." She tried to look casual, and failed utterly. "A guy."

"Oh?" Things had been pretty quiet on the guy front for CJ

since the debacle last year with Josh Johnson. She hadn't shown an interest in any of the guys in our year at school, though more than a few had made it clear they were ready to fall at her feet whenever she said the word. CJ had that kind of effect on guys.

"Which guy?"

"You don't know him. I met him last night." A secret little smile played around her mouth.

"At the movies?"

She'd gone with Ashleigh and a couple of other girls. I didn't think there'd been any guys involved.

"Yeah. We had pizza together afterwards."

"What's he like?"

"Nice. You'll see when he meets us at the markets."

Great. I already knew how this would play out. Love-struck guy, utterly smitten with CJ's undeniable beauty, would fawn all over her while she laughed and flirted and they both completely ignored me. Fun times.

I was definitely going to need back-up.

Chapter Three

I tried Zac first. I was aching to see him. Maybe he wasn't the greatest dancer, or the hottest-looking guy in school, but to me he was perfect. Just one look into those gorgeous dark eyes and I was lost. He had a way of listening that made me feel as if I was the most important person in the world.

He was a long time answering the phone, and sounded sleepy when he came on the line.

"Hey, gorgeous. Want to come to the markets with me and CJ?"

He snorted. "Go shopping? With your *sister*? What time is it?"

"It's after ten. Did I wake you?"

A huge yawn was my answer. "Didn't get to bed until late."

"So how about it? Come with us?"

"I can't believe you woke me up to ask that. Do I *look* like a masochist?" He sounded grumpy. That wasn't like him. It must have been a really late night.

"Sorry. I just really want to see you."

"Well, I can't. I've got an essay due tomorrow, and Dad will skin me alive if I get another C. I'll see you at school tomorrow."

I stared at the phone after he'd hung up. Well, that was abrupt. And so unlike Zac.

Fortunately, Sona didn't let me down. That girl never missed a chance to go shopping.

Sydney put on another gorgeous summer day. The sun was so hot it had me wishing I'd worn a long-sleeved shirt, even though I would have sweltered. I could feel it biting at my arms already as we headed down George Street towards the markets. With my pale skin, I'd be fried within twenty minutes, despite the sunscreen I'd slathered on.

Sona had no such trouble, of course. Her beautiful dark skin never burned. That was one advantage of Indian heritage over Irish. Another, according to CJ at least, was the thick black rope of hair that hung down her back, past her butt. CJ would have killed for hair long enough to sit on. Me, I was just happy if I could get my curls to act like hair instead of orange steel wool.

We met Sona on the corner of George and Argyle.

"Hi!" She gave me a brief but enthusiastic hug, as if she hadn't seen me in years, though we'd been at school together on Friday. She smelled of her usual floral perfume, with a hint of Indian spices underneath. I always had the best food when I went to Sona's for dinner. Her mum was a fabulous cook.

"Hey, Sona," said CJ, who was scanning everyone who walked past. Probably looking for her new man.

"Hey, CJ." Sona tucked one arm through mine. The other was carrying a bag from Galaxy bookshop.

"You already been shopping?" I asked.

She grinned. "Can't come to town without checking out Galaxy. They had the new Iron Druid book." She opened the bag to let me peek in.

I was pretty keen on Galaxy myself. Science fiction and fantasy was my thing, and I'd never lived anywhere before that had a whole bookshop devoted to it. But lately I hadn't been reading as much. Guess you didn't need to read fantasy when your life supplied enough of it.

The markets were straight ahead, set up in the middle of the street, which had been closed to traffic. There were people everywhere; many of them tourists shopping for souvenirs, but a lot of locals, too. You could find all sorts of treasures here among the tourist crap, and afterwards there were plenty of bars and restaurants to take your money if you wanted to just sit and watch the world go by for a while. Not that we'd be hitting the bars, of course, though CJ at least could pass for over eighteen. Cafés were more our style. I could just imagine the hysterics Sona's mum would have if we got busted trying to buy alcohol.

A band was playing somewhere nearby—part-rock, part-country, part-what-the-hell-it's-Sunday-afternoon—and the crowd had a relaxed feel. Lots of smiling faces, little kids with ice cream, bigger kids with that bargain-hunting gleam in their eye.

"Are we looking for something in particular?" Sona asked as we headed into the crowd.

"CJ's new boyfriend, apparently."

CJ was forging on ahead, but she heard that. "He's not my boyfriend. Not yet, anyway."

Sona's dark eyes gleamed with interest. "What's this? New man? When did this happen?"

"Last night at the movies. Apparently they fell in love over pizza. Who knew anchovies could be so romantic?"

Sona snorted. "How come when I go to the movies I only meet bozos who want to talk on their mobile phone all through the show?"

"Maybe you're going to the wrong kind of movie?"

"What movie did she see? Was it that new Brad Pitt one? God, that looks so depressing. Hey, CJ? What movie was it?"

But CJ wasn't listening any more. She was striding eagerly toward a guy lounging by a stall that sold printed T-shirts. He had black hair that fell messily around his face—either he hadn't brushed it or he'd spent an hour in front of the mirror with the hair gel to get it to fall in such a carefully casual way. His eyes were as blue as CJ's, or my own, and they lit up now with a smile as he caught sight of her.

Sona stopped dead in her tracks. "Wow. Is that him? That guy is *hot*."

I had to admit she was right, but then, that was hardly surprising. CJ only dated guys that looked like male models. This one wore faded blue jeans and a shirt whose cut-off sleeves displayed tanned muscles. Nice.

"What's up?" Sona asked when I didn't reply. "You don't like him?"

"No, it's not that. I was just trying to think where I'd seen him before. He looks familiar somehow."

"Yeah, *hello*. That's because he looks more like her twin than you do." She cast me a quick guilty look. "No offence."

She was right. If CJ were a boy, this was exactly what she would look like. Talk about made for each other.

"None taken. I've got eyes, haven't I? I'm well aware that we don't look much alike."

Make that "anything alike". Apart from our eyes, which were the same blue as Dad's, we had nothing in common. She was tall; I was short. She tanned easily, where I freckled and burned. Her black hair rippled like silk down her back, and my out-of-control curls were that shade of red that's really orange. Arty types called it "Titian"; everyone else called it "carrot".

To add insult to injury, CJ had curves in all the right places. The best you could say about my figure was that it was "athletic". No wonder people often mistook her for my older sister. We were both seventeen, nearly eighteen, but CJ could pass for early twenties, while people often assumed I was much younger, because of my height. Or lack of it.

She stepped in close to him, and he draped one muscled arm around her shoulders and leaned his forehead against hers in an oddly tender gesture. Had she really only met this guy last night? She usually played a lot harder to get in the beginning. CJ was a big believer in "treat 'em mean, keep 'em keen".

He looked up and noticed us lurking hesitantly in the background. "You must be CJ's sister."

"That's me. I'm Violet, but my friends call me Vi." Too soon to say whether he would be one of them.

"Oh." CJ looked around, as if noticing we were there for the first time. She had it pretty bad. "This is Aaron. Aaron, this is my sister and her friend, Sona."

"Hi, Sona. You two won't mind if I borrow CJ for a while, I hope?"

"Um, sure," I said. "Borrow away."

He flashed a magazine-worthy smile, then took CJ's hand in his and drew her away through the crowd.

"Wow," Sona said. "Wonder if he's got any brothers?"

I laughed. "As if your parents would let you go out with anyone who wasn't Indian."

She smiled dreamily. "For him, I'd elope."

We started moving through the market again, following the general direction that they'd taken. I stopped to check out a stall selling old black-and-white photos of Sydney, but my mind wasn't fully on what was in front of me.

"I wonder how old he is?"

"Who? Aaron?" She looked their way. We could just see the tops of two dark heads, leaning close together over some trinket or other. "Older than her, I'd say. He doesn't look like he's still at school."

No, he didn't—but then, anyone meeting CJ for the first time would probably think the same. They certainly made a good-looking couple. But I still preferred Zac, with his hair flopping in his eyes and his dubious dance skills. Not to mention the cute dimple that peeked out when he smiled. I knew he'd always have my back. Lately that seemed a lot more important than a pretty face. I hoped he'd got over his grumpiness from the morning, but I wasn't going to fret about it. I had enough on my plate without making up new things to worry about.

"What's that smell?" Sona drew in a deep, appreciative breath. "I'm starving."

She followed her nose to a stall that sold roasted nuts, where she bought some cashews, and we munched as we walked. A harsh squawking made me jump, but it was only two seagulls squabbling over a piece of bread on the ground. For a moment there it had sounded like a crow.

I'd been wary of crows and ravens ever since last year and our run-in with the Morrigan, whose birds they were. Any flash of black in the corner of my vision could make me jump these days. Even finding a black feather on the ground made my skin crawl with the feeling of being watched. Ravens might not sound that terrifying, but when you've stood on the steps of St Mary's Cathedral and looked out at the huge plaza in front of it, and every scrap of that whole enormous space is covered in black feathered bodies—thousands and thousands of the little bastards, all staring at you with those beady little eyes—then you discover a fear of black birds damn fast.

But there were none to be seen today, so I kept my paranoias to myself and followed Sona through the markets, stopping now and then to check out anything that looked interesting. Sona bought herself a pair of silver earrings that dangled like miniature chandeliers when she held them up to her ears. I debated over candles that smelled like coconut and lime, but decided in the end that they'd just make me hungry every time I lit them, so I left them there.

Sona was still looking at candles, so I moved on to the wind chimes next door, running my hand along their metal tubes just to enjoy the bell-like tones they produced. CJ and Aaron were at the next stall, a table piled high with a whole lot of antique-looking stuff like candelabrae and old plates covered in painted roses. Not my kind of thing, but I saw Aaron pick up a slightly tarnished-looking hand mirror and show its ornate back to CJ. He whispered something to her and she laughed and nodded.

My hackles rose as I watched him pay the stallholder and hand it to CJ. He was gorgeous—too gorgeous—and now he was giving her a gift? So much for not worrying.

"What are you doing?"

CJ turned in surprise at my hostile tone, the smile fading from her face.

"What do you mean?"

"Are you seriously going to let him give you that? Have you forgotten what happened with the last gift we received?" I glared at Aaron, who glanced between the two of us, apparently bemused. But all Sidhe were good actors.

She stepped closer and spoke through gritted teeth. "Will you keep your voice down? What is your issue? Aaron's human."

"How the hell do you know? You only met him last night. Don't you think it's rather convenient that he looks exactly like someone you'd fall for? It's like he's tailor-made as bait!"

"Excuse me?" said Aaron.

Sona hurried over from the candle stall. "What's going on?"

"CJ's trying to get us both turned into frogs," I said bitterly. How could she be so stupid? I'd had enough of fairy gifts. Couldn't she see what was happening here?

"Vi's flipping out over nothing," CJ said at the same time, trying to simultaneously glare at me and smile reassuringly at Aaron and ending up looking like she had a facial tic.

"It's not *nothing*. If you weren't so bloody vain, you'd see that."

People were staring at us, but I didn't care. This was way too important. I glanced around uneasily. We were in danger just being this close to a Sidhe. Now I wished we still had Simon shadowing us as a bodyguard, like he'd done last year when it all blew up.

What could I do? I had no weapons, no access to aether. My eyes fell on the wind chimes I'd been so happily ding-donging only moments before. Steel had iron in it, right? And iron had caused plenty of damage to Puck last year, when the warders had chained him with it.

I snatched a set of chimes off the rack, in a great discordant clanging of sound. The stallholder yelled a protest but I ignored him. With quick strides, I closed the distance between me and Aaron and shoved the jangling pipes at his gorgeous face.

"What the hell?" He pushed me away, but I pressed the metal firmly against his bare arm, bracing myself for the sizzle of burnt flesh.

"Vi, for God's sake!" CJ's face was red with fury and embarrassment. In the background Sona was hurriedly assuring the owner of the wind chimes, that yes, I did intend to pay for them; but I was intent on Aaron.

He finally succeeded in wrestling me off and I checked his arm. No burn marks.

Either the Sidhe had some new protection against iron, or the guy was human after all. I glanced around at the watching crowd and my cheeks began to burn.

"Happy now?" CJ hissed.

"Your sister's nuts," Aaron said. "If this is your idea of a fun time … I don't need this kind of shit."

He stalked off. CJ shot me a filthy look and ran after him, leaving me to patch things up with the wind chime seller. My face flamed as I handed over the money and he bagged the chimes for me, still shaking his head.

"Well, that was exciting," Sona said.

"Don't start."

"At least I got some bargains. I even got a free sample from the candle maker."

"Congratulations."

We walked back past the candle stall. There was such a confusion of scents that it was almost too much. I could still make out the yummy coconut and lime smell, but there was something else there that reminded me too much of burnt toffee.

It's just a candle, you idiot. I was so jumpy I was seeing Sidhe everywhere, and now I'd managed to assault that poor guy with a set of wind chimes for nothing. I'd be lucky if CJ spoke to me inside a week. Sometimes an active imagination could be a pain in the butt.

Chapter Four

Our great plan to infiltrate the restricted section of the library had to be put on hold. For the first time since we'd been using the library, someone was actually in there.

We closed the library door behind us, then stopped short at this unusual sight. The restricted area was its own glassed-off room at the back of the library, and Gretel was inside, pulling books from the shelves to add to an ever-growing pile she had on a table by the door.

"What the hell is she doing?" CJ muttered.

I rolled my eyes at her. "I don't know, ballroom dancing?"

Too late, I remembered I'd resolved to be extra nice to my sister, to make up for that horrible scene at the markets earlier.

"But no one ever comes in here except us." She sounded like a sulky child who didn't want to share her toys. At least she was talking to me, though barely. When I'd asked what had happened with Aaron, she'd just turned her back and refused to answer.

"Clearly that's not the case any more." Gretel had the door

to the restricted section shut, so she hadn't heard us come in. "I wonder what she's looking for? I bet the restricted section is getting a workout lately, with everybody trying to figure out how to deal with the Sidhe."

"I don't care what she's looking for. I'd rather know what she's *finding*."

Gretel was so engrossed in her search that she didn't realise we were there until we opened the door of the restricted section and let ourselves in. She looked up sharply as the door creaked.

"You shouldn't be in here," she said.

"We just wondered what you were looking for," I said.

"Maybe we can help," CJ added.

We'd never been in here before. The air had a strong old-book smell. Some of the things on the shelves were so old they weren't even books. I saw scrolls there, stacked in neat pigeonholes. I longed to get my hands on one and unroll it. Would I find a map? Or a spell? Or something written in hieroglyphics?

Gretel gathered up her pile of books. "I'm finished. Let's go."

Reluctantly, we followed her out of the forbidden room. She placed the books on another table outside, then locked the door behind her and slipped the key into the pocket of her jacket. Damn. So much for my hope she might accidentally leave it unlocked.

"Let me help you with those." CJ took the top few books off the stack, but somehow managed to knock the rest of them off the table in the process.

"Be careful!" Gretel dropped to her knees on the carpet, a look of horror on her face. "Some of these books are hundreds of years old."

CJ passed her books to me then leaned over Gretel to help. Gretel didn't look as though she wanted any more of CJ's help, but eventually all the books were regathered and cradled protectively in Gretel's arms.

"What are you researching?" I tried to read the spines, but half of them were in other languages, and most of the others were too faded to make out from a brief sideways glimpse. I caught something about transfiguration, but that might as well have been in another language, too. That was something about changing bodies, right? So maybe she had a lead on Dad's situation. It was about time somebody did.

"These are for your mother. She has a new theory on your father's curse."

CJ snorted. "A new theory? We've had plenty of those. What we need is less theories, more action."

"We've all been working as hard as we can—"

"But it's not enough, is it?" CJ was the same height as Gretel; she stood toe to toe with her, glaring as if Gretel were personally responsible for turning Dad into a bear. "Dad's gone. He slipped away while you guys were mucking around with your books and your gadgets and your damned experiments. It might already be too late to get him back."

Gretel clutched the books tighter to her chest, as if they could shield her from CJ's anger, but CJ had already whirled and stormed out of the library.

Maybe I should go after her. "Sorry," I said to Gretel. "She's a bit wound up today."

Gretel sighed. "I don't blame her. There's nothing worse than feeling helpless. We've all tried everything we could think of, but we may as well have sat around twiddling our thumbs for all the good it's done us. Your dad and Warder Nabukov are no better off than they were four months ago."

That's right. I tended to forget about poor Sergei, trapped as a fairytale ogre. At least he could still talk. I opened the door for her and walked with her down the corridor towards Mum's office.

"CJ thinks we should be using the treasures. Fighting magic with magic."

Another sigh, this one even bigger. "Maybe we could have, if we still had the cauldron. I blame myself."

"What for?"

"If only we'd set up the condensors differently that day, we might not have lost the cauldron."

"You can't blame yourself for that. They were hardly optimum working conditions. If you hadn't come when you did, God knows what would have happened to CJ and the rest of us." The Morrigan had been out for blood by that stage. "You saved us, Gretel. You shouldn't feel guilty."

"Maybe. I just keep thinking there must have been a better way." She gave a bitter laugh. "I guess that's why I'm a computer tech and not a seeker."

"I've never understood how the cauldron got to Sydney in the first place," I said. "It was meant to be safe in Paris. Dad even went there and saw it. Then, the next thing we know, it's here in Sydney disguised as a Spartan jug. Did the Sidhe go to Paris and swap it over? But why didn't they just take it then? Why spell it to look like something else and wait until it had travelled all the way here before they took it?"

We arrived at Mum's office. I knocked on the door, since Gretel's hands were full. When there was no answer I let her in, and she dumped the heavy pile of books on the desk with a sigh of relief. Mum's desk was already covered in papers and books, as if she was leaping from project to project with no time to clean up in between.

Gretel leaned against the desk, flexing her fingers with relief after lumping the heavy books around. "No Sidhe could have got to Paris. There are no openings from their prison into the northern hemisphere. Someone who escaped here would have had to travel there, and there wasn't enough time between the first breakout and the time the cauldron was discovered in the Art Gallery for anyone to travel to Europe by sea."

"But they could have flown."

She shook her head. "No, they couldn't. Sidhe can't travel by plane—too much iron and too little space. They must have used a human agent to go to Paris and make the switch."

"But why didn't the human just steal the cauldron straight off, then?"

"Well, they could have. But then the whole warding community would have been tipped off that something was up, and they might have been caught before they got back to Australia with it. Much smarter to do it the way they did— switch it for something spelled to look like it so as not to arouse suspicion, then wait for the Louvre to deliver it here as part of their travelling exhibition."

I cleared a space and sat on Mum's messy desk. The office smelled of stale food, as if she'd been eating too many meals in here. We hardly saw her any more. It was like losing both parents at once.

"But who could it be? It's got to be someone in the organisation, surely. But everyone's got an alibi. Who's been to Paris lately?"

Gretel folded her arms across her chest. "I'm not sure I should be talking about this with you. Maybe you should ask your mother."

"Oh, come on, Gretel! This is my dad we're talking about. What's the point of keeping secrets any more? How does that help anyone?"

She sighed. "Fine. Well, there's the Paris staff, of course, though how the Sidhe could have contacted them is anyone's guess. But they all checked out clean. Then there were half a dozen people from Australia who'd been to the Paris offices in the last six months, including your parents. They were all clean too. The only other person who'd been to France recently enough was Kerrie Davidson, and she didn't even go to Paris."

Quite apart from the fact that she was the first person to be hit with a fairytale curse, which ruled her out as a Sidhe sympathiser.

"So basically everyone's got an alibi, and we're back where we started."

"Pretty much, yeah. And yet someone must have done it."

"Did you test everyone with your truth serum stuff?"

"Absolutely. We weren't taking anyone's word for anything. But they were all telling the truth."

"God. That's so frustrating."

"Tell me about it." She blew out a long breath. "Anyway, I'd better get back to work. Oh, hi, Warder Winters."

Mum came in just as Gretel was leaving. Damn. I'd been

hoping to get a little peek inside those books. Mum looked at the pile of books on the desk and sighed.

"I don't think I'll be able to have dinner with you girls tonight after all. I've got too much work on. Just grab yourselves something from the kitchen."

"That's okay." We were pretty used to eating alone these days. I slid off the desk and walked to the door. She was already seated, with the first book open in front of her. I don't think she even noticed when I slipped out and closed the door behind me.

I contemplated calling Zac—I needed someone to talk to. But he'd been so short with me this morning, it might be better to wait until I could see him face to face. Probably better to find CJ and see if I could make amends for the incident at the markets. I felt like such an idiot.

There was no sign of her in the guest suite we shared when we stayed here, though there was the usual evidence that she'd been here—clothes all over the floor and makeup covering every flat surface in the bathroom. Next I checked the staff kitchen. Ronnie was the only one there, and she said she hadn't seen CJ. I even tried Dad's room, but the seeker on duty in the little anteroom said she wasn't there, and I felt too miserable even to peek in on Dad.

So I went back to the suite and flicked on the TV to pass the time. I'd barely kicked my shoes off and put my feet up before the door crashed open and my twin burst in, waving something triumphantly. She seemed to have forgotten she was mad with me.

"What have you got there?"

"A key."

"A key to what?"

"Only to the restricted section in the library."

"*What?*"

She grinned as I sat up straight, my feet thumping back down to the floor. "I sneaked it out of Gretel's pocket in the library. I dropped those books to distract her, then took it when we were picking them up. She was so worried about the precious books she didn't even notice."

"But what if she notices now? You've got to give it back."

"Relax. This is a copy. As soon as I got it, I ducked out and got a duplicate cut. The original's back in her pocket already. She'll never know."

"Wow. I never knew you were so good at being bad."

"Ha!" She grinned at me. "You ain't seen nothing yet."

"Damn," said CJ. "Why couldn't they put a lock on this door?"

"Keep your voice down!" I pushed her into the library and shut the door behind us. "Do you want everyone to know what we're up to?"

She glared at me. Clearly I wasn't forgiven yet. As usual, we had the place to ourselves. The only sound was the low hum of the air-conditioning.

"We could shove one of those tables against the door."

"That wouldn't look at all suspicious." I eyed the restricted section, locked behind its glass wall at the back of the big room. It was in direct line of sight from the main door. If someone did come into the library while we were in there, there would be no hiding. It was a risk, but ... "We'll just have to get in and out as fast as possible and hope no one comes in while we're doing it."

"All right then." She marched over to the restricted section and inserted her key in the lock. "Let's do this."

I half-expected an alarm to go off as she opened the door, but that was just my guilty conscience talking. It wasn't a large room, but there could have been as many as a thousand books in it, filling two big sets of shelves, and then there was the big section full of scrolls on the back wall. Those fascinated me, but I was almost afraid to touch them. Some of them looked so old I worried they would crumble away to dust in my hands.

"You take that side," she ordered, "and I'll start over here."

My heart sank as I began scanning titles. All the ones on the top two shelves were in German.

"Small problem," CJ said. "These are all in another language."

"Which one?"

"Maybe Latin?" I heard her slide a book out and start flipping pages. "It's got that many pictures of body parts it must be an anatomy textbook."

"Why would it be in the restricted section if it's an anatomy textbook?"

"I don't know." Her tone was frosty. "Maybe it's so old it's valuable."

After the German shelves, the books switched to French. I knew a little French, but only the basic "where is the bathroom?" and "this is the pencil of my aunt" kind, so I didn't bother pulling those out, either. I moved on to the next bookcase, but I couldn't even recognise the lettering on those. It was some kind of squiggly script that made no sense to me. Fortunately, the squiggle books only filled a single shelf.

After that they stopped putting titles on the spines at all. I scanned the remaining books on this side, but none of them had anything written on them apart from a set of numbers at the very bottom. Some kind of magic-library code? How the hell did they find anything in here?

I pulled out the first one and groaned.

"What's your problem?" CJ asked.

"Do you want the good news or the bad news?"

"Let's take the good news."

"I found one in English."

She came round to my side. "Then what's the bad news?"

"It's handwritten. Looks like some kind of diary."

She pulled half a dozen at random from the shelves in front of me, flicking through each in turn. They were different shapes and sizes, and the handwriting varied widely, often within the same volume, but they were all the same kind of thing. Diary entries.

"This one's got pictures." She tipped the book she held to show me a drawing of a hideous woman with long straggly hair and pointed teeth. It was labelled "Ban Sidhe" in neat printing beneath it. "Ban Sidhe? Hey—banshee! I want to read this one."

"We're supposed to be looking for something about artefacts that might help Dad," I reminded her.

"I know that." She put it back in its place and we both moved around to the other side. Here we finally found some books with English titles, but nothing that screamed *hey, read me, I'll help!*

"*A Guide to the Herb Lore of the Ancients.*" CJ trailed a finger along the spines and read titles aloud. "*A Historie of Faerie Weaponry. Dissertation on the Mutability of Time.* What the hell does mutability mean?"

"Umm. Something about changing, I think? Or not changing? No, wait, that's 'immutability'. Grab that weaponry one. Could be something in there."

She passed it to me, and took one for herself that seemed to be a history of the wars between the great families of the Sidhe. "Maybe it'll have something useful about the four treasures."

We locked the door behind us and I sighed with relief as I settled into an armchair with my forbidden book. We'd made it this far without getting caught. We each kept another book from the main library open on our laps as we read, just in case someone came in and wanted to know what we were reading.

"This guy's handwriting is almost impossible to read," CJ complained after a few moments. "Look at this! Is that supposed to be an 's'? Cause it looks more like an 'f' to me."

The ink had also faded so much in parts that it was barely legible. She snapped the book shut in frustration and let her head thump against the back of her chair.

"We are never going to find anything in there! There are too many books. We could be reading for a year. And what if the information we want is in another language? It's hopeless."

"What's hopeless?"

My head turned so fast I almost gave myself whiplash. I hadn't even heard the door open, and there Kerrie stood in the doorway, looking enquiringly at us.

"Oh, nothing." CJ recovered faster than I did. "I was just complaining about this assignment I've got."

Kerrie came closer, a sympathetic smile on her pretty face. "Is that what you're studying for?"

"Yeah. You know what Year 12 is like."

She laughed. "Yeah, it's not so long since I was there myself. I still have nightmares where I'm going into the Maths exam and I realise I haven't studied any of the right topics."

"What have you got there?" I gestured at the book under her arm, trying to distract her before she looked too closely at our "study".

"Just returning something for Warder Kincumber." She held up a familiar key, then headed over to the restricted section.

While she was unlocking it I slid the book I'd been reading under my seat cushion. CJ dropped hers on the floor and kicked it under her chair. We both watched Kerrie replace her book on the shelves then relock the door behind her. She'd put it back near the beginning of the section where the untitled books began, the ones that all seemed to be diaries.

She looked a bit surprised to find us both still staring at her when she turned around.

"So, what's happening with you two? Just study, study, study?"

"Can't wait for the holidays," CJ said.

She laughed. "I bet."

"I heard you had a holiday recently," I said, seeing an opening.

"Well, it was a bit short for a real holiday. I went to France for four days. My boyfriend's cousin was getting married, and we flew over for the wedding."

That was odd. Simon had kissed her awake because she didn't have anyone else who loved her enough to break the spell.

"I thought they said you didn't have a boyfriend when you got hit with the Snow White curse?"

"Yeah, we broke up not long after that trip." She smiled. "But we're back together now. It all worked out in the end."

"France is a long way to go for four days," CJ said.

"Tell me about it." She grimaced. "Twenty-four hours on a plane. I don't recommend it. We would have liked to stay longer, but he couldn't get any more time off work."

"Did you get a chance to do much sightseeing? Did you go to Paris?" I asked.

"No. We flew into Marseilles on the Friday night. The wedding was Saturday night, then Sunday we borrowed a friend's car. Saw Avignon and Orange. Monday we went to Lascaux and saw the cave paintings there. Twenty thousand years old. Amazing. Tuesday we headed back and flew out that night. Talk about a whirlwind trip."

"You must have been exhausted."

"Yeah, it was pretty tiring. Still, it was better than nothing. France is a beautiful country. You ever been there?"

"No, but I'd love to go one day."

"Better start saving then! I'll catch you guys later."

"See you."

CJ waited until the door closed behind Kerrie, then raised an eyebrow at me. "What was all that about? You best buddies all of a sudden?"

"Gretel told me that Kerrie was in France last year. Maybe she's the traitor."

"So? You think if you ask her what she did on her holiday she's going to tell you she had a lovely time in Paris stealing the cauldron?"

I shrugged, feeling a bit defensive. "I don't know. I just

wanted to see the look on her face. See if I believed her or not."

"And did you?"

"I don't know," I said again. "Did she seem like she was telling the truth to you?"

CJ yawned. "I wasn't really paying that much attention. Hey, too bad for Simon, eh? She's got a boyfriend."

"Yeah." That was bad news. Although I knew someone who might not think so. Gretel still seemed to get awfully tongue-tied whenever Simon was around.

CJ stood and stretched so hard I heard something crack in her back. "At least she didn't come in when we were in there looking at the books. That could have gotten ugly."

She wandered over to the locked door and pulled out her key again.

"What are you doing?"

"I want to have a look at that book she returned. See what old Dorian's been reading. Do you remember which one it was?"

I got up and went with her. "It had a bluey-grey cover. Must be that one."

The others on the same shelf all had red or brown covers. Most were leather, but this one was some kind of cloth, like linen, stiffened with lacquer. CJ opened it to the first page. There was no title or author; it just launched straight into a long, rambling description of the writer's travels between farms, on the trail of something called a pookah, which was causing mischief. The date at the top of the page said "June, 1692".

"What's a pookah?" CJ asked. "Is that like Puck? Is he talking about Puck?"

We'd met Puck last year. He'd been the first to escape the

Sidhe prison. I'd certainly have classed him as mischievous—or even downright dangerous—but what the writer was describing sounded much less human. In any case it didn't seem like anything that could help us.

"I don't know. Look, that page is dog-eared. Maybe that's what Dorian was looking at."

She flipped to the page with the turned-down corner. This one was dated 1701, and looked like it had been written by someone else. At least his—or her—handwriting was easier to read.

I took the book from her and read:

I heard of a young man who was travelling around the county healing the sick by the laying on of hands. In the town of Kilkenny I met a widow who swore that he had saved her child from the pox. The lad in question was a sturdy child of three summers, whose ruddy cheeks spoke of rude good health, but the boy's mother swore that he had been on his death bed not a se'en-night before. This stranger had come to her house as the priest was giving the child the last rites and cured him simply by laying his hands on the boy's chest. She said the pox faded from his skin even as she watched, and then the lad sat up and asked for food.

I spoke to the local priest and he told a different story, that the child had not been so very sick after all, and had been cured by the power of prayer, but I am not inclined to believe him. I have heard many similar reports, and believe the young man may be a powerful latent, whose natural affinities could be harnessed to great good if given the proper training. I fear for his safety, however, if he continues upon this course. Already he has been driven from several towns, decried as a witch. Alas, some folk's fear of things they do not understand leads them to violence, whether good or ill is intended. This young man is a danger to himself and also to us, as long as he remains at large.

"Go on," said CJ. "What happened then?"

"I don't know." I turned several more pages, but there was no further mention of the young man with healing hands before the book ended. "It doesn't say."

"Some stupid farmer with a pitchfork probably got to him. Or else they burnt him at the stake."

"I don't think they were still doing that in the 1700s."

"Well, whatever." She lost interest in the possible fate of the faith healer. "Do you think someone like that could heal Dad? Is that why Dorian was interested?"

"Maybe. Or maybe he was reading a completely different part of the book. Either way, it doesn't really help us, does it?" I closed the book and replaced it on the shelf, feeling suddenly exhausted. "We don't have anyone capable of healing with the laying on of hands, or any aether to fuel that kind of magic."

"A Sidhe could probably do it, if we could capture one."

Catching a Sidhe was so unlikely I didn't bother answering. Her shoulders sagged; she looked as dispirited as I felt. We locked the door behind us and left the library. I didn't know about CJ, but I was starting to feel like there was a reason no one had found an answer before us, and it was simple.

There wasn't one.

Chapter Five

It was a relief to get on the school bus on Monday morning. School—at least now that the Morrigan wasn't masquerading as a teacher any more—was a safe haven of normality. Fretting about essays and homework seemed almost comfortable compared to the kind of worries I had in the rest of my life.

As usual, the driver took off before most of the people at my stop had found a seat. I almost fell into Sona's lap.

"Hey," she said. "Nice of you to drop in."

"Ha ha."

"Are you okay? You look kind of down."

"Just tired."

Sona knew a lot more about the situation than most. She'd been there at the cathedral with me, fighting to save the cauldron from the Morrigan, so I knew I could trust her with the truth. But that didn't mean I had to burden her with every miserable detail.

She was silent for a moment, but nothing stopped Sona talking for long. "Did I tell you about the heels I got for the party? I didn't think Mum would let me have them, but she said, 'Sona, you are nearly eighteen. You are old enough now to make your own choices, and if you choose to spend your whole party with aching feet, it is up to you.'"

"Wow. Have aliens taken your mother and wiped her brain? She really said you were old enough to make your own choices?"

"I know! Crazy, right? But it's only a pair of shoes. I bet if I asked her if I could go out with a boy it would be a different story."

"Some things never change," I agreed.

The bus stopped again and the doors ground open. And speaking of boys … My heart lifted as Zac got on and moved down the aisle toward us. His hair flopped messily into his eyes, and my fingers itched to stroke it out of the way.

"Hi." He let his hand brush across my arm in a tender gesture as he took the seat across from me. He wasn't big on public displays of affection, so there were no morning kisses on the bus, but that brief touch of his hand said *hi, I'm here for you.*

He, too, had been there, standing shoulder to shoulder with me against the Morrigan. I confided in him even more than I did in Sona.

"Hi!" I said. "I tried to ring you last night, but I couldn't get hold of you."

"Yeah. Sorry about that. We had kind of a family conference until late."

"Really? What about?"

For the first time I noticed that he wasn't looking too happy himself this morning. Some girlfriend I was, too caught up in my own worries to notice his. The pause stretched so long I thought he wasn't going to answer, then he shook his head.

"Tell you later."

Sona's ears immediately pricked up. "Why? Is it a secret? I can stick my fingers in my ears if you like."

Which she did, chanting "la, la, la," at full volume. The kids in the seat in front turned round to stare, but she ignored them. They were only Year Sevens. They giggled, but soon lost interest.

"It's not a secret. It's just … complicated." He gave her an impatient look. "Will you shut the hell up?"

She took her fingers out of her ears and eyed him speculatively. "Your parents have won the lottery and you were all trying to decide how to spend your millions. No, wait, I know! Your little brother announced he was gay."

He glared at her. His usual good humour seemed to be missing in action this morning. "Seriously, Sona?"

"Don't tell me your parents are getting a divorce?"

"Sona!" I hushed her, but Zac dug his earphones out of his bag with a grim look and made a point of inserting them and turning his back to us. "Leave him alone. I think he's upset about something."

"Oh, well. You'll just have to kiss him all better." She ignored my frown and changed the subject. "Have you decided what you're wearing to my party yet?"

I shrugged. "I don't know. I haven't really had time to think about it."

"Violet! The party is this Saturday. I spent all last night making the perfect playlist. You'd better start thinking about it real soon. You are not allowed to turn up in your jeans. My mother would be horrified."

"I thought your mother had turned over a new leaf."

"We are talking about clothes here. Indian women take their fashion very seriously. This is no laughing matter."

I snorted. "You sound just like my sister."

She was still harassing me when the bus pulled up at school, but I managed to shake her off and catch Zac's arm as we passed the admin block.

"Hey! Are you okay?"

"We need to talk." He glanced at his watch. "No time now, the bell's about to go. Meet me at lunch, okay?"

The bell started ringing, and he leaned forward and pressed his lips against mine in a brief kiss, then jogged away in the direction of his first class. I stayed there, frowning after him.

It was never a good thing when your boyfriend said "we need to talk", right? That usually meant he wanted to break up with you. And he'd been strange on the phone on Sunday morning, too. I touched my mouth, feeling the warmth of his kiss lingering there. But he never usually kissed me in public, so that was a good sign, wasn't it? Or was he just trying to soften the blow, and I should prepare myself for the "it's not you, it's me" speech?

I hardly heard a word Mr Dunkley said in Physics, and English wasn't much better. I didn't have any classes with Zac until Ancient History after lunch, so I stewed all through the first four periods.

Hey, at least it took my mind off Dad.

By the time I met him at our usual spot under the trees in the grassed area behind the canteen, I'd worked myself up into such a state I was shaking. I sat on the seat next to him and pulled my lunch out of my bag, but that was as far as I got. The thought of actually eating anything made me feel physically ill. A ball of worry the size of a small moon had lodged itself inside my ribcage, and the sombre look on Zac's face wasn't helping any. How could I stand to lose him too? With Dad gone, Mum disappearing into work, and CJ more than half not talking to me, Zac was my lifeline.

He was quiet, working his way steadily through a ham sandwich, but I couldn't stand the waiting any more.

"So. Your family conference last night." I tried to sound casual, as if my whole world wasn't hanging in the balance. "What was that all about?"

He put his sandwich down, staring at it as if surprised to find someone had been eating it. "Yeah. It was interesting. Dad kind of sprung one on us."

For a moment I was afraid Sona was right and his parents were getting divorced. "He's leaving your mum?"

"No!" He looked up sharply. "Nothing like that." He sighed, and took my hand. It was still shaking, but he didn't seem to notice. "You know Dad works for this big overseas company, right?"

"Right."

"Well ... they've offered him a promotion. The chance to be head of a whole division."

"But?" Obviously there was a but involved.

"But it's in London."

"London?" Oh, no. The small moon suddenly ballooned to the size of a planet. I couldn't lose him now, not on top of everything else. "You're moving to *London?*"

It was so far away. I'd never see him again.

"No! Well, maybe. I don't know yet."

I waited, heart pounding. His grip on my hand was uncomfortably tight, but I wasn't letting go.

"Mum and Dad said they'd talked about it for ages. They'd weighed up all the pros and cons, and they thought it would be good for us as a family to experience life in another country. And everything's so close over there. You can hop on a plane and be anywhere in Europe in a couple of hours. We could do a lot of weekend trips, really see the world."

Unlike when you lived in Australia, and Europe was twenty-four hours or more away, as Kerrie had discovered. Australia was a great place to live, but God, it was a long way from anywhere.

His brown eyes were so serious. "They're definitely going, and taking the little two. But they said they weren't sure what to do about me. Mum's worried about taking me out of school now, with the HSC coming up. They have a different system over there, and who knows if I could even get the same subjects if I just turn up partway through the final year." He took a deep breath. "So Dad said they would leave the decision to me. I can go with them and finish school over there, or I can stay here, finish the year off, and then join them."

Wow. All of a sudden everyone's parents were trusting them to make their own choices. Except mine, of course.

"They'd let you stay here on your own?" I could hardly bear to hope, but the anxious mass lodged beneath my ribs began to melt anyway.

"I could live with Uncle Mike and Auntie Alice. They're only a couple of suburbs away, and they have a spare room. They said they wouldn't mind having a kid around the place again. All my cousins have moved out."

I leaned in close and put my arms around his neck. He smelled of sunshine and whatever washing powder his mum used on his shirts. He was warm and solid, and the only decent thing in my life right now. How much more could I bear to lose?

"Hey, it's okay." His lips tickled my ear, his breath warm on my skin. "Don't be upset."

"Don't be upset? How can you say that? I know you can be annoying sometimes, but I'd kind of miss you. I'd probably even miss your terrible dancing." I tried to make a joke of it, but the tear that leaked from the corner of my eye gave me away.

He wiped it away tenderly. He had a way of looking at me that made me feel special, like his attention was a giant spotlight, focused on me and nothing else. His brown eyes were warm and caring, but there was something else there too. Something that looked a lot like indecision.

"I don't want to leave you." A bird squawked in the tree above us, a harsh sound. I looked up. Bloody crows. "But I'm not that close to my uncle and aunt, and I'd miss my family."

"You could live with us."

"I don't think your parents would allow that, even if mine did."

"Why? Mum wouldn't care. She's hardly ever home anyway." I'd *make* her agree. I couldn't let him go.

"I don't know, Vi. It's such a big decision. I just don't know what to do."

"Please don't go." Tears began to roll down my cheeks again, and I let them fall. "I couldn't bear it."

He crushed me against his chest, and I hid my damp face against his shirt and listened to the steady rhythm of his heart.

"I almost wish Mum and Dad had told me I had to go." His deep voice rumbled against my ear. "The other two don't have to make any big decisions, they just do as they're told."

A crow hopped down to the grass not far away, watching Zac's abandoned sandwich with beady eyes. I shuddered, wishing I had a nice big rock to hurl at it.

Why did everything have to keep changing? And why were all the changes for the worse? If Zac's dad were here, I could cheerfully have thrown a nice big rock at *him* for doing this.

I scrubbed the tears away. The bell would be going for the end of lunch soon, and I didn't want everyone to know I'd been crying.

"I know this is a tough decision." I tried to sound grown-up and understanding, but inside me a hurt child was screaming *but why? Why is it a tough decision? Don't you love me?* "But I really need you right now."

"I know. I know you do."

The crow hopped closer. Swift as thought, Zac snatched a pebble from the ground and hurled it at the bird. It screeched and took off over our heads, so close the wind of its passing ruffled my hair.

"I hate crows," he said.

Chapter Six

As the days passed and her party got closer, Sona got more and more excited. She was like a little kid. You'd have thought it was her eighth birthday, not her eighteenth. She was practically jumping out of her skin by Friday afternoon, babbling about the music she'd chosen and what everyone she knew was wearing, and filling my head with the names of a hundred Indian dishes that would be on the menu. I was kind of glad I wasn't seeing her at all on the Saturday before the big night. I wasn't really in a party mood, and it was a little hard to act all excited and interested when every time I saw Zac the serious look on his face broke my heart just a little more.

We didn't talk any more that week about the big move. On one hand, I felt kind of bad about pressuring him to stay, but on the other, every day that passed made me feel a little more hurt that he was so obviously tempted to leave. We were pretty quiet in the car as he drove CJ and me to Sona's party on Saturday night. It was being held at a restaurant in Crow's Nest called The Lucky Elephant, owned by one of Sona's many aunties. Naturally it was an Indian restaurant.

If CJ noticed the silence in the car she didn't comment. She was back to not really talking to me, since it was clear by now that Aaron wasn't changing his mind and coming back. Looked like I was well and truly off the "favourite sister" list.

The elephant on the sign of The Lucky Elephant was blue and looked drunk, his trunk curled up like a question mark and his eyes gazing two different directions at once. We could hear music pounding from the restaurant as soon as we pulled up outside, strange Indian music that wailed like a seasick cat being strangled. That didn't sound much like the playlist Sona had been fussing over all week. This could be an interesting night.

We went inside and were hit with a wall of sound, as what seemed like a hundred voices competed with that atonal music. Sona saw us and waved, her eyes fever-bright. She looked like a million dollars in a red sheath dress whose bodice sparkled with gold. The red shoes she'd gotten so excited about made her taller than CJ.

"Hi!" Sona's voice squeaked with excitement. If I hadn't known her parents so well, I might have wondered if she was drunk. "Come and meet everyone."

She tucked one hand through my arm and one through Zac's, and dragged us around the room. CJ saw another friend from school and escaped, but Zac and I got introduced to every member of Sona's considerable family.

"It's like an explosion in a chocolate box in here," Zac muttered in my ear.

"They're beautiful!" I whispered back. Most of the Indian ladies were wearing saris in a range of bright colours, heavily ornamented with gold or silver thread. They certainly knew how to dress for an occasion.

There seemed to be an endless parade of smiling sari-clad aunts and enormous-eyed cousins, and I quickly gave up hope of remembering even a single name.

"Of course, that's only the Australian parts of the family," she said when we finally ran out of extended family. "There's a lot more in India, but my grandmother was the only one who came out for the party."

We hadn't been introduced to any grandmothers, so I guessed she hadn't arrived yet. "Is that the one that always complains because you can't speak Hindi?"

"No, that's Dad's mum. Naaniji is Mum's mum. She's cool. She had to come out for work anyway. It was just lucky the timing fitted in with the party." She glanced at her watch. "She said she had to finish up a meeting, but she should be here soon."

There was a burst of laughter from the family milling around the entry, and Sona's face lit up. "There she is!"

I looked over and did a double-take at the small woman standing there surveying the room. She was wearing an elegant gold sari, but her thick grey hair was pulled back in its usual bun, and even though I hadn't seen her since last year I knew her instantly.

It was Dena Bhutra. Warder Bhutra.

"That's your grandmother?"

"Yes! Come and say hello." She grabbed my wrist and towed me through the crowd and around the tables. Dena watched her come with an indulgent smile.

"Sona, my darling! You look so beautiful! So grown-up!" She kissed Sona warmly and smiled at me. "Who is your lovely friend?"

So that was the way she wanted to play it. Didn't she know that Sona knew all about my involvement with the warders? Dena had definitely been in Sydney when Kerrie woke from her curse. Had she already gone home before my big showdown with the Morrigan? I couldn't remember, so I gave a mental shrug and played along as Sona introduced us, pretending I'd never met her.

At dinner, Zac and I were at a table with Sona, a few of the guys from the robotics club, and some of Sona's female cousins. Conversation was a little awkward at first, but once the food came things improved. The Indian girls had a great time laughing at us Westerners gulping water to ease the burning of the curries.

"These are mild!" said one, a pretty girl with huge brown eyes made to look even larger by the amount of eyeliner she'd used. "You should try the ones we have at home."

My mouth was on fire and I had to keep blinking tears from my eyes. Sona took pity on me.

"Have some yoghurt. It'll help." She passed me a bowl and I took some gratefully.

Apart from the heat, the food was delicious. I tried a little of everything and, long before dishes stopped arriving at the table, I was full. God knew how these girls kept their figures if they ate like this every night. Maybe the curry burned all the fat away.

When the meal was finished, someone turned the music off. Sona's dad tapped the microphone and winced at the noise it made.

"Oh, no." Sona rolled her eyes. "He's going to make a speech. I *told* him not to. I just want to dance!"

Mr Desai beamed at the assembled guests and said something in Hindi which got a few laughs.

"Dad! Speak English. You know I don't speak Hindi."

"That is why it is a good language to talk about you in, Sona." There was more laughter, and he cleared his throat. "Ladies and gentlemen, family and friends, welcome to this wonderful restaurant where we celebrate Sona's eighteenth birthday. Thank you to my sister-in-law Indira and her husband for the beautiful meal we have just enjoyed. I hope you are all enjoying yourselves?"

There was a chorus of agreement. "That is good. I just want to say a few words about my lovely daughter on this special occasion. Doesn't she look beautiful tonight? I remember very well the night she came into this world, eighteen years ago. I can tell you she was not very beautiful then. In fact, she had so much hair that at first I was afraid my wife had given birth to a monkey."

"Dad!" Sona groaned and buried her face in her hands.

"But now look at her! She has grown into a lovely young woman." He smiled down at his wife, still seated at the table beside him, and took her hand. I felt the sting of tears in my eyes, and it wasn't from the curry this time. "We are very proud of you, Sona. You are a sweet girl, a dutiful daughter, and a good friend. You have worked very hard at your studies, and we wish you every success and happiness as you begin your adult life."

"And we hope you find a nice Indian boy to marry!" one of the aunties called out.

When the laughter and applause died down Mr Desai called Sona up to the front table. Someone pressed play on the music again and "Happy Birthday" started up. From the kitchen two waiters carried out the most enormous birthday cake, with eighteen sparklers fizzing away on top. Everyone got to their feet and sang while Sona's mum and dad hugged her and I tried very hard not to cry.

Mr Desai's face as he looked at Sona was so proud and happy. I would be eighteen soon, but my dad wouldn't be at the party. If we even had one. He wouldn't be able to make nice speeches and tell me how proud he was of me. He might never speak again. I might never get one of his special bone-crushing hugs again, or hear another one of his lame dad jokes. He couldn't walk me down the aisle at my wedding or even finish teaching me to drive.

I glanced across at CJ, to see how she was taking this moment, but she had her back turned rather pointedly to me. I sighed. Funny how I'd never properly appreciated our happy family until it was gone.

The dancing started after Sona cut the cake. Thankfully it wasn't Indian music any more. Sona was the first one on the floor, but the Indian aunties weren't far behind. They certainly knew how to party. If Sona's feet were hurting in those skyscraper heels, she showed no sign of it.

I moved into Zac's arms a little stiffly. I was bursting to know what he was thinking. Had he decided? But at the same time I was afraid to ask, in case I didn't like the answer.

"How are things going at home?" I asked. That seemed like a safe enough compromise.

"Dad flew out on Wednesday. He's going to look around at houses and schools for the brats." *And maybe for Zac?* "Though he said he might be too busy with the new job to do much until Mum gets over there."

"When is your Mum going over?"

"She's taking the kids out of school at the end of the week. Says there's no point mucking around once you've made up your mind. She's already booked the company to pack up all the furniture and stuff, and spoken to a real estate agent about renting the house out."

"That doesn't give you much time to decide."

He gazed down at me, his face grave. "I've already decided."

My heart sped up. I had to hold it together, whatever he said. I couldn't ruin Sona's party by bursting into tears on the dance floor.

"And what's the decision?"

"That the girl I love needs me, so I'm staying."

Tears welled in my eyes. "Oh, thank God."

He smiled. "Hey, don't cry. You're supposed to be happy."

"I am! But what did your parents say?"

His face clouded over. "I think Mum was hoping I'd go. But I told her I thought it would be too disruptive to leave now." He grinned, and the dimple made its appearance. "I didn't want to tell her the real reason—that some pretty girl has me wrapped around her finger."

I sagged against him, relief making my knees weak. "Shall I ask them to put on 'YMCA' to celebrate? I know how much you love it."

He grinned, leaning close to be heard above the music. "That's fine. Don't go to any trouble on my account."

"Oh, it's no trouble."

I left him and danced closer to Sona, giddy with relief. Now I could relax and enjoy the party. Maybe he'd still leave when the HSC was over, but that seemed like such a long time away. Anything could happen between now and then.

Sona caught my hands and whirled me around. She loved to dance, and looked like she was having the time of her life. She had personally picked every song on the DJ's playlist.

"Hey!" she shouted as we spun. "Isn't that your bodyguard guy? What's he doing here?"

I looked round and saw Simon in the doorway. She'd been calling him that ever since the toads and diamonds episode last year, when he and Kyle had escorted me and CJ to school. "I'd better go see what he wants."

When I got to him he was leaning over, talking to Warder Bhutra. She looked up, her usual calm expression marred by a frown.

"Is something wrong?" I asked. "What are you doing here?"

He glanced at Warder Bhutra, and she said, "Simon's here to give me an update on the situation."

"What situation?" Had something gone wrong at headquarters? Was it Dad?

"They've detected a build-up of aether."

"Where?"

"Here," said Simon. "Or near as we can tell, anyway. Warder Winters is concerned another attack may be imminent. I need to get you and your sister, and Warder Bhutra, to safety."

Safety. He was kidding, right? Was anywhere safe any more? CJ and I had gone to sleep in our own beds one night, perfectly fine, and woken up the next morning spitting frogs and diamonds with every word. Sergei—Warder Nabukov—had gotten on a plane in Tokyo a man and arrived in Sydney an ogre. Another fairytale attack could hit anyone, any time. The walls of headquarters were no defence against magical attack.

Clearly Dena Bhutra felt the same.

"I appreciate Warder Winters' concern," she said, "but I didn't fly all the way from Mumbai for my granddaughter's birthday party only to run out halfway through. If my family is in danger, I'd rather stay and see if I can be of help."

Simon's frustration showed on his face. "Ma'am, your family may only be in danger *because* you are here. It seems certain you are the Sidhe's objective. If you leave now you may very well be saving your family."

She gazed across the room, taking in the groups still talking and laughing at the tables, and the heaving mass of bodies on the dance floor.

"Did you bring a Hendrix counter with you?"

"Yes, but I can't very well bring it in here among all these civilians."

"Of course you can." She smiled at him. "Most of the adults are drunk, and the children are all too wrapped up in each other and the music to pay you any attention. Besides, several members of my family know all about the work we do. They can help you. Geva!"

She signalled to one of the aunties who was seated at a nearby table. Looking like an exotic flower in her hot pink sari, Geva rose and came over to us.

"Yes, Mama-ji?"

Quickly Dena explained the situation, and sent Geva out with Simon.

"How many of your family know about the warders?" I asked, watching Sona spin without a care in the world.

"Not many. We only tell the latent ones."

"But CJ's not latent," I objected without thinking.

Her eyes narrowed. "And how do you know that?"

Oops. We'd found that out snooping in the records, but I wasn't going to own up to that.

"No, CJ's not latent," she continued, when she realised I wasn't going to answer, "and therefore she would never have heard a whisper of the truth if she hadn't been hit by that curse last year. After that it was a little hard to hide it from her."

"But she's my twin."

I meant that I could never hide anything from her, but Dena mistook my meaning.

"It's possible for even close relations like yourself to have different levels of magical potential. I have eight children, but only three of them show any latency. Those three have all been introduced to our world and given training. One of them will take my place as a warder when I die. My other children will go to their graves thinking their mother nothing but an eccentric old woman who liked to collect the folk tales of her country."

I sat down next to her, easing my feet in their strappy sandals. God knew how Sona kept dancing in those ridiculous heels. I liked high heels as much as the next girl, but I liked being able to walk even better. She was still going, flicking her long dark hair as she danced, and I watched her while we waited for Simon and Geva.

"What would have happened then, if you didn't have that many children? What if none of them were latent? Who would be the next warder?"

The words were out of my mouth before I realised they were more applicable to myself. Mum and Dad were both warders, but they only had one latent child—me. Who was going to replace the other one of them if CJ couldn't? And what if Dad never recovered? Did that mean I'd have to become a warder in his place?

"It doesn't have to follow in a direct line. One of my brothers could take the job, or one of their children. A cousin, even. As long as a descendant of the original warder takes the role, the chain isn't broken."

Okay, then. Maybe one of my uncles or aunts was going to get called up one day. Most of them lived in the UK, so I didn't see them very often, and I hadn't thought to ask Mum if they were already involved with the warders.

Sona was dancing in the centre of a big circle now. Many of the dancers in the circle clapped and cheered as she gyrated among them. I saw CJ laughing, next to some of the guys from the robotics club. Looked like the Indian girls had finally managed to get them up on the dance floor.

"Why didn't you want Sona to know I already knew you?" Simon and Geva hurried in, Simon carrying a small book-sized box with an odd glass tube attached to it. It was a Hendrix counter, used for measuring the presence and strength of aether, the stuff of magic. Geva casually draped the dangling end of her sari over it to hide it from anyone not looking too closely. "She knows all about the warders now. She met the Morrigan last year."

Dena, too, was watching her daughter and Simon as they moved slowly around the room. "Sona knows the warders exist, and of your connection with them. She has no idea that her own grandmother is one, and that her family has been involved since the organisation was founded." She shot me a severe look. "And since Sona has no more latency than your sister, I would prefer it to remain that way. Bad enough that nearly a quarter of the world now believes in magic, without spreading our business any further."

"A quarter of the world? Really?"

I saw a flash of pink from underneath the folds of Geva's sari. That wasn't good. The room was dark, and coloured lights were flashing from the dance floor, so it was hard to be sure, but if the Hendrix counter was picking up aether here we could be in for trouble. Dena frowned, and I wondered if Simon had any portable condensors in the car.

"According to Gretel's program, anyway. She's been monitoring the spread of belief since the attacks began last year." She rose to her feet. "It's just as well we already have the Sidhe confined."

I rose too, concerned at the worry on her face. "What do you mean?"

"If our ancestors were trying to forge their great prison now, they would never have succeeded. Remember, the Sidhe thrive on belief. It gives them power. The level of belief in the world today would make the Sidhe too strong. They were only vulnerable because the Industrial Revolution weakened them. There was so much iron in the cities that the lesser Sidhe, like the brownies, who had often lived closely with people, couldn't enter. In the Age of Steam, it was easy to deny that they'd ever existed. But the levels of belief we're seeing now are far higher than they were then."

That didn't sound good. Did that mean if they managed to break free now we'd never get rid of them again?

"Excuse me," she said. "I must go and check ..."

She marched off toward Simon and his assistant, who had now arrived on the edge of the circle of dancers. I caught another flash of light from under the concealment of the sari, much stronger this time, and a chill stole over me. I hurried after Dena.

"Sona!" she called. It took a couple of attempts to get Sona's attention, with the noise of the music. Sona had the strangest look on her face as she spun in the centre of the circle. Just watching her made me feel dizzy. "Come here!"

Sona danced her way across the floor, and the circle parted to let her through. She stepped onto the carpet, and kept dancing, though she no longer looked like she was having fun. She winced as she jiggled and shimmied toward her grandmother. I knew she shouldn't have worn those shoes.

Dena caught at her hand and pulled her toward Simon. He glanced surreptitiously at his readings and I saw the strong red colour of the light from the Hendrix counter.

"It's coming from *her*," he said.

"Sona!" Dena sounded almost cross, but I think she was alarmed. "Stand still."

Sona continued to bounce from foot to foot, swaying and shivering. Her dark eyes were wide and frightened. "I—I can't."

Dena grabbed her by the shoulders and tried to force her to stillness. "What do you mean you can't? Are you drunk?"

"Naaniji!" Tears started in her eyes. "I haven't drunk anything. But I can't stop—I can't stop dancing!"

We all looked down at her feet. At the red shoes. Oh, shit. The hairs on the back of my neck prickled. Red shoes. One of Hans Christian Andersen's darkest fairy tales.

Sona was crying openly now, and people nearby were starting to realise something was wrong. Simon thrust the Hendrix counter into Dena's hands and swept Sona up into his arms. But her feet continued to move, kicking and jerking, her whole body spasming.

"We've got to get her out of here," he said, and Dena nodded, her face a sickly colour in the flashing lights from the dance floor. Sona turned her face against Simon's shoulder and sobbed like a little child, too frightened to understand what was happening to her.

But we knew. The fairytale curse had struck again.

Chapter Seven

"What is the matter?" Mr Desai appeared at Dena's elbow, his face tight with alarm. "What is wrong with Sona?"

He gestured at the DJ, and the music cut off abruptly. The party came to a sudden stop, and Sona's mother cried out in shock at the group gathering around her daughter.

"Get her out of here," Dena ordered Simon. He nodded and began forging a path to the door.

Mr Desai stepped in front of him. "Where is this man taking Sona?" Panic bubbled just below the surface. He tried to grab Simon's arm, but Geva stopped him.

"It is all right, Rajit," said Dena. "He is with me. We will get help for her. Simon, go."

"But what is wrong?"

Someone turned the lights back on full and we blinked at each other. The disco lights, still flashing, seemed inappropriate now. Sona's mum pushed through the crowd to her husband's side.

"Come, Rajit. We must go with Sona." Her eyes were frightened, too, but Dena nodded approvingly. For the first time I wondered if Sona's mum was one of her three latent children.

"This way." Dena shepherded them before her, and they were gone before most of the guests realised what was happening.

Zac appeared at my side. "What's going on?"

Worried relatives milled around us. Bursts of agitated Hindi came from all sides. Geva stood in the middle of a storm, waving her hands and trying to placate everyone. I left her to it and tugged Zac toward the door.

"We have to go. Sona's been attacked by the Sidhe."

His expression was grim. "Where are we going?"

"Headquarters. In The Rocks."

"What about CJ?" he asked as we stepped out into the warm night. It was much quieter out here.

I hesitated. Even if she wasn't talking to me, I didn't want to leave CJ stranded, but I was desperate to get to Sona. I blew out a quick, frustrated breath, but just as I was about to plunge back inside in search of her, she followed us out.

"What the hell was that all about?" she said as we got in the car. "One minute we're dancing, and next thing I know everyone's weeping and wailing about Sona. What happened to her? I couldn't make any sense out of what they were saying."

"It's another fairytale attack," I said.

"Shit." Yep, that about summed it up. "Which one?"

"The Red Shoes." Bloody Hans Christian Andersen. Why did all his stories have to be so damn miserable? Serve him right if I went and vandalised his stupid statue.

"What's that one about?"

"The usual misogynistic crap. Girls can't have any fun. This poor girl gets a pair of beautiful red dancing shoes, and her punishment for the crime of maybe actually enjoying herself for once is that she can't take them off. She has to keep dancing until she drops dead of exhaustion."

That last part came out a bit squeaky. Would Sona die if the warders couldn't figure out a cure? How long did she have?

Zac took one hand off the wheel and gave my leg a comforting squeeze. "But why was Sona hit? I thought all the other people who've been targeted have been connected with the warders?"

I glanced over my shoulder at CJ. She shrugged, as if to say *it's up to you if you want to tell him*. Of course I wanted to—and I had no doubt I could trust him—but Dena hadn't even wanted Sona herself to know of her connection with the warders. She probably wouldn't be too keen on me telling my boyfriend.

"Is it because she's your friend?" he asked me.

"Could be."

I looked out the window. We were almost there: The Lucky Elephant was in Crow's Nest, so the city was just a short drive across the Harbour Bridge. The illuminated night city was beautiful, but I had no appreciation for it tonight. I willed Zac to drive faster as we came down off the bridge and wound through the back streets toward headquarters.

The steel gate was usually down across the entrance to the parking garage at this time of night, but it stood open. Dena's car had probably just come through.

"Just drop us here," I said, impatient to get inside.

He looked a little deflated. "You don't want me to come in with you?"

"Better not." Tempers and emotions would be high in there, and no one would be happy at me dragging in an outsider. I leaned over and kissed him in apology. His lips were warm and sweet. "Thanks. You're the best."

I got out and slammed the door. He leaned across and lowered the passenger side window. "Will Sona be all right?"

CJ just looked at me over the roof of the car. We both knew that was a question that was impossible to answer.

"I don't know," I said. "I'll ring you as soon as I hear anything."

That would have to be enough. He nodded, but I didn't stay to see him drive away. We took the lift straight to level 1, pretty confident we knew where they would have taken Sona.

Sure enough, I could hear raised voices as we approached Kerrie's old room. It had originally been an office, but they'd set it up more like a hospital room when Kerrie was there, locked in her undead sleep, and I doubted anyone had had time to change it since. It seemed like a good place for our newest patient.

I opened the door, and found the room crowded with people already. A flood of outraged Hindi greeted me. Mr Desai was waving his arms at Dena, who faced him with her usual calm, while Sona's mother alternated between scolding him and sobbing over Sona, now lying deathly still on the bed. She was covered in a white sheet, and her normally dark skin had an unnatural pallor.

Mum was there, too, and a couple of people I didn't know. One of them was inserting a drip into Sona's arm. She murmured something to Simon, who was helping her, and he looked up and saw us.

In three quick strides he crossed the room. "Girls, please wait outside."

His bulk blocked my view of the bed, and I strained to see around him. "I want to see her. She's my friend."

He took my shoulders in a firm grip, turned me around, and all but shoved me out the door.

"Simon, please! I have to make sure she's all right."

He closed the door behind us, shutting out the noise and the view. He looked cranky. "Of course she's not all right. What's the matter with you? You should know better. Do you think her parents need you poking your nose in? They're having enough trouble coping as it is."

I flinched, and felt the sting of tears.

"Sorry." He rubbed a hand across his eyes. "I'm just tired. And sick to death of this shit. But there's nothing you or anyone else can do for now. Leave Dena to deal with the parents and come back tomorrow. It's late."

"She's not moving any more," I said. "Is she asleep?"

"They had to put her under, she was too distressed."

"So when she wakes up she'll start dancing again?" The thought horrified me. Sona loved dancing. It seemed such a cruel joke. And what about the shoes? Was she still wearing them?

"I'd say so. We couldn't get her shoes off." Well, that answered that question. "They'll try to keep her sedated as much as possible. We can hydrate her and feed her intravenously."

"Yeah, but not forever."

He didn't answer that. "Go to bed, girls. There's nothing you can do here."

He went back inside and shut the door in my face. I glanced at CJ, but she just shrugged.

"Might as well go to bed, I guess. My feet are killing me."

Her feet were killing her? What about poor Sona? I glared at her back as she headed down the corridor towards our room.

Before I could follow, the door opened again and Mum came out. She gave me a tired smile. It was a pretty half-hearted effort.

"What a week. I can't believe it. First the news about Rebecca, and now this!"

Rebecca? I racked my brain but drew a blank. "Who's Rebecca?"

"Dorian's wife."

I blinked. "Has she been attacked too?" Funny that I hadn't heard anything.

"No." Mum sighed, a sound of deep exhaustion and despair. "Her cancer's back, and the doctors have given the poor woman only a couple of weeks. They said she'll be lucky to see out the month." She shook her head. "Dorian's beside himself."

A couple of weeks! No wonder Dorian had looked so haggard when I saw him in the vault the other day. The poor bastard. Fancy having that hanging over your head. It made me feel even more guilty than usual for not liking him.

Mum scrubbed at her face, just as Simon had a minute ago. No one around here was getting enough sleep.

"I feel so helpless. There's nothing we can *do*." She caught my odd look. "Oh, not about Rebecca. Obviously we can't do anything if the doctors can't. I mean all the rest of it. Dad, Sergei—and now poor Sona. Do you realise that now, with Dorian so distracted with Rebecca, Frida is the only warder left who's not coping with a personal crisis? One by one, we're being targeted."

And who knew how much longer she'd keep that status, the way things were going? I didn't say it, but I'm sure Mum was thinking it anyway.

"We need your father," she said, and her face twisted as if she was about to burst into tears.

I threw my arms around her and squeezed hard. "I know, Mum. We all miss him."

"He was always the creative one." She hugged me tight and spoke into my hair. "I'm just an administrator. That's why they picked me to succeed Grandma, you know. They could have chosen your uncle, but I have a real flair for organisation." She sounded almost bitter about it, as if a flair for organisation was shameful. "My latency was the bare minimum to be a warder. Your father's is much higher. Nothing like Dorian's, of course. Poor Dorian."

Her voice softened again. Yes, poor Dorian. And Rebecca. I wouldn't want to be either of them at the moment.

She looked down at me, her eyes suspiciously bright. She was a good height for hugging, so much taller than me that I could still snuggle in under her chin like I had as a kid. I should remember to hug her more often. We could both do with a few hugs. I just never seemed to see her any more.

"You know, if Dorian had been born in the days before we banished the aether from the world, he could have been a great mage. His latency scores are phenomenal."

Latency scores. God, I was sick of hearing about them. Everyone in this place was obsessed with them. As if it meant anything any more. How good you *might* have been, if only there was enough aether in the world. Who cared? CJ was all riled up about hers, and it meant nothing. There wasn't enough aether and that was that. Might as well get all excited about who might have been the best mammoth hunter if only we were all still living in caves.

Besides, who wanted to live in a world where Dorian Kincumber could do magic? He was insufferable enough as he was.

Mum sighed. "And then he might have been able to do something for Dad, or poor Sona. Still, no point wishing for that, is there? We'd all be in far worse straits if magic was loose in the world again. The Sidhe would be turning people into bears or whatever they damn well pleased all over the place, like in the bad old days."

"Never mind, Mum. I'm sure we'll work something out."

I wasn't sure of any such thing, but she seemed like she could do with some encouragement. She was babbling, and that was a sure sign she was stressed.

She smiled. "Listen to me, going on. What's the time?" She looked at her watch. "Good God, you should be in bed. Where's your sister?"

"Probably in our room."

"You should join her. We'll get Emmet to look at Sona in the morning. He might have some ideas."

When Dad had made collars last year to stop CJ and me spitting frogs and diamonds with every word, they'd eventually stopped working; it was Emmet who had fixed them. He was a smart guy with a flair for coming up with clever solutions, but I had a feeling he wouldn't be able to fix this.

I said goodnight to Mum and headed back upstairs. Our

guest suite had a small lounge area, with four bedrooms opening off it. Dena would probably be staying in one at the moment. As I came into the main room, I could hear CJ talking in the bedroom we shared when we stayed here overnight. And from the gooey tone of voice, it sounded like maybe Aaron had changed his mind.

I opened the bedroom door, ready to leave if she gave me a dirty look. She flinched and dropped something on the bed. But it wasn't her phone.

It was the mirror Aaron had bought for her at the markets.

"What are you doing? I heard you talking to someone."

It couldn't be, could it? It lay there on the bed, innocently reflecting the ceiling. Could I have been right after all? But if Aaron was a Sidhe, why hadn't the iron marked him?

"No. Just talking to myself." She opened her blue eyes wide, in that I'm-so-innocent shtick she'd been pulling since we were both small. I hadn't believed it then and I didn't believe it now.

"And laughing at your own jokes? And using your special gooey talking-to-boys voice? Pull the other one."

"I do *not* have a gooey talking-to-boys voice." She threw me an offended look.

"Oh, you *so* do. What were you doing with that mirror?" I felt sick. What was she tangled up in now?

"Nothing." She shoved it half under her pillow, as if I'd forget it if I couldn't see it.

"Show it to me."

"No." She threw herself down on the bed, arms wrapped protectively around the pillow, and the mirror beneath. "It's late. Turn off the light."

Chapter Eight

When I woke up next morning I had that awful feeling that something was hanging over me, but I couldn't think what. Dad? Sona? No, wait—what the hell was going on with CJ and that mirror? I cracked an eyelid. CJ was still asleep. I'd have to wait until she got up.

Well, that wasn't going to fly. CJ could have won an Olympic medal if they'd had a sleeping event, and I had things to do. I picked up a shoe and threw it across the room, then quickly feigned sleep. I heard her stir.

In a minute I was rewarded by the sound of her getting out of bed and heading to the bathroom. Quietly I slipped across the carpet and groped under her pillow. It was still there, cold and hard.

It didn't look like much. The surface was tarnished; it was obviously old. There was even a spot on the handle where the carving had been worn by many years of hands gripping it. I looked into it and saw nothing but my own blue eyes and worried face reflected back at me. Was it enchanted? I'd have to get it checked out with a Hendrix counter to be sure. It looked disappointingly ordinary at the moment, but that didn't prove anything.

"What are you doing?" CJ crossed the distance from the door to the bed in two angry strides and made a grab for the mirror. "Give me that."

"What is this?" I danced back, waving it like an accusation in her face. "He's enchanted you, hasn't he?"

"Who?"

"Aaron."

"What are you talking about?" She made another grab for it and I hid it behind my back. "Don't be ridiculous."

"I heard you last night. You were talking to Aaron through this mirror. Don't lie."

"Oh, for God's sake. What is your problem? I was on the phone."

"Crap. You were holding this, not a phone. I'm not blind."

"Crap, yourself. And you *are* blind. The phone was on the bed. I had it on loudspeaker." She snorted. "Talking through a mirror. As if. What am I, Snow White's stepmother? 'Mirror, mirror, on the wall.' Sorry, but we're fresh out of magic mirrors around here."

"Crystal Jane Riley. If you don't tell me what's going on right now, I'm taking this mirror straight to Mum, and you can try your bullshit on her."

She glared at me, but when I made to walk out the door she sighed and sank down on her bed.

"Fine. Have it your way. But you better not screw this up."

I stared, a little confused. "So it *is* a magic mirror?"

"Yes." She tilted her chin in that defiant way I'd been seeing since childhood. "But I wasn't talking to Aaron."

I stared at the mirror in my hand. Only my own rather wild blue eyes looked back at me. Even though I'd been accusing her of hiding this from me, it still kind of caught me by surprise that it was true.

"Then who were you talking to?"

"His name's Ariel."

Figured. With CJ there was always a guy involved.

"What happened to Aaron?"

She shrugged impatiently. "*You* happened to Aaron. I haven't seen him since you threw that wobbly at the markets. Forget him. He's not important."

"But he gave you the mirror."

"Yeah, well, he's human. Someone else must have set it up. Ariel didn't say how, just that he wanted to talk to me."

I sat down next to her, feeling lost. "What does he want to talk to you about? And why are you even talking to a Sidhe? What if he enchants you?"

"He won't enchant me. Relax, would you? We're only talking."

"But why?"

"Isn't it obvious? So I can use him to get what I want. He can help me turn Dad back."

I groaned and fell back on the bed, covering my eyes with my hands. "CJ, you can't trust a word he says. Why would he help you turn Dad back?"

"He won't know that's what he's doing." She leaned over and grabbed my wrists, hauling my hands away from my eyes. Her blue gaze was very serious. "Vi, give me a little credit. I know the Sidhe can't be trusted. I'm not stupid. He thinks he's suckering me, but he's going to wake up one day and find that I've suckered him instead."

Oh, God. This just went from bad to worse. She thought she could out-trick the original tricksters?

"This sounds like a really bad idea."

She blew out an impatient breath. "I knew you'd think that. That's why I didn't want to tell you."

"This is so dangerous, Ceej!"

"Will you stop panicking? Yeah, it's a bit risky."

"A *bit*? Do you even have a plan?"

She stood up, hauling me up with her. "I don't see why I should tell you if all you're going to do is pour cold water on everything."

"Somebody's got to be sensible."

"The time for being sensible is past. How much progress have the warders made, being *sensible*? Do you ever want to see Dad again?"

"Of course I do."

She shoved the mirror under her pillow. "Let's go and get some breakfast. Maybe you'll feel braver with some food inside you."

I followed her out the door, vaguely insulted. I was brave. I could be plenty brave when I had to be. Objecting to outright lunacy didn't make me a coward.

We headed down the corridor towards Sona's room.

"Why do you think the attacks have started again?" I asked.

"I don't know if that's the right question. Maybe a better one would be why did they stop in the first place?"

"Dorian reckoned it was because time moves differently in their world to ours. Maybe no time at all has passed for them."

"Or maybe they've been busy cooking up some nasty surprise in the cauldron. It's supposed to be able to produce anything you wish for, isn't it?"

"Well, there's limits." I grasped the door handle of Sona's room and paused. Gretel had tried to explain it to me after our big showdown with the Morrigan, but I hadn't been paying all that much attention. After all, the Morrigan had just whisked the damn thing back to fairyland with her, so it hadn't seemed all that important any more. Whatever it could or couldn't do, it wouldn't be doing it for us. "It stands to reason there must be, otherwise they'd just have wished themselves out of prison already."

She shuddered. "God, that's a terrible thought. But think, Vi. If we still had it, we could wish up a cure for Dad. And Sona."

"And Sergei. Don't forget him." What was the point of wishing we still had the cauldron? It was gone, and there was nothing we could do about it.

Kyle looked up when I peeked round the door of Sona's room. "No visitors, girls."

"We just wanted to see—"

"There's nothing to see. No change." He made shooing motions at us, and I closed the door, feeling like a five-year-old.

We stood in the corridor and stared at each other. "Who do you think will be next?" CJ asked. "Now that the attacks have started again, I bet Frida's feeling nervous."

I nodded. I hadn't met the seventh warder yet. She'd been in Sydney just after we'd been attacked last year, but not since. "Maybe if she stays away she'll be safe."

"Dad wasn't, was he? Or Sergei."

Or Sona. When had they gotten to her? "True. I don't get how that works. Dad was in France, and Sergei was in Japan. I thought the aether was only leaking in Australia. It's like the cauldron. How did they get to it in Paris?"

"We should check the screen." They had a big screen in the monitor room, like something out of a disaster movie. Every time we went in there I kept expecting someone to shout "call the president". Usually it displayed a map of the world that tracked the levels of aether. "Maybe the leaks spread and they didn't tell us."

"Maybe." It certainly wouldn't be the first time the warders had withheld information from us. We took the lift down to the ground floor.

There were ten or twelve staff on duty when we went in but only Ronnie said hello. She was tapping away at her keyboard as if her life depended on it. Columns of numbers streamed across her screen. I had no idea what she was doing but it looked impressive.

The big screen was disappointingly blank.

"What's happening with the aether?"

"I can get that up for you," she said.

The map of the world appeared. Except for Australia, the world glowed a calm green. In the land down under things weren't looking so rosy. Or rather, they were too rosy. Red splotches had broken out all around the circumference of the continent, with a particularly big dirty one centred over Sydney.

"No change, then."

"Not really." She sounded much cheerier about it than

anyone had a right to be, but then Ronnie was so caught up in her computers that she sometimes lost sight of what it all meant in the real world. She was probably just excited about the data stream working right. "Do you want a close-up of that?"

"No. we're good." It hadn't changed much since the breakouts began last year.

"I heard about that girl they brought in last night," said Ronnie. "Dena's granddaughter. Poor little chick. What a terrible thing."

"Yeah." She had no idea. For someone who loved dancing as much as Sona did, it was a cruel trick.

"She was pretty unlucky."

"How do you mean?"

"Oh, you know, just that Dena's got a big family. Her odds of being picked must have been something like two hundred to one. Could have been anyone else, but it was her. Like I said: unlucky."

I stared at her. Just unlucky? Or was there more to it? *Did they pick Sona because she's your friend?* Zac had asked last night, and I hadn't answered, because I hadn't wanted to tell him about Sona's connection to the warders through Dena. But what if it was true?

I swallowed hard and turned away, staring at the big screen without really seeing it. What if this was personal? What if the Morrigan was on a targeted vendetta? She'd already had a go at me and CJ. Next it had been Dad. Now she'd attacked Sona, when she could have had any one of Dena's numerous relatives, or even Dena herself. What about Geva, Dena's daughter, who was already involved with the warders? Or her other two latent children? Why had she picked Sona?

Sona, who was my best friend. Sona, who'd helped us defy the Morrigan at the cathedral. And there was one other person who'd been there too, standing side by side with us against her. One other person intimately connected with me.

"What's wrong?" Ronnie asked. "You look like you've seen a ghost."

"Nothing. I'm fine."

Not a ghost. A damn Sidhe. My stomach clenched with fear. Would Zac be the next victim? How could I protect him? The truth was I couldn't. If they could get to Dad in Paris, and Sergei in Tokyo, how could anyone be safe?

I turned abruptly to Ronnie.

"Did anyone ever figure out how they got to the cauldron in Paris?" It seemed politer than asking straight out if they'd figured out yet who'd betrayed them. "Gretel said the Sidhe couldn't have travelled there, and they couldn't find anyone who might have had access."

"No," said Ronnie, "it's still a mystery, but we did manage to pinpoint when it must have happened. There was a false alarm over there in September."

"What kind of false alarm?"

"Well, as it turns out, probably the kind that isn't false at all. But at the time they assumed it was a false alarm. The Louvre experienced a brief interruption to the power supply on the alarm system, but when our people over there checked it out, the cauldron was unharmed and nothing had been taken. We now think that must have been when whoever it was made the switch."

"Was this alarm just on the cauldron?"

"It covered the whole room in which it was stored, but yes, just that section."

"You'd think that might have made people suspicious."

Ronnie shrugged. "You have to remember that we've been guarding this thing for a couple of centuries, and at that stage no one had any reason to suspect the Sidhe might be loose. The most they would have been worried about was mundane theft, and since the cauldron was still clearly there, we assumed there was nothing to worry about."

"When exactly was this? September, you said?"

"That's right." She referenced something on her screen. "September the fifth."

I tried to remember when Kerrie had said she'd been in France. Had she told me?

Back in the corridor, CJ raised an eyebrow at me. "Why are you still obsessing over who got to the cauldron? It really doesn't matter now, only the fact that they did."

"Don't you care who the traitor is? It matters if they're going to help the Sidhe steal back the stone or the spear or the sword. It matters that we don't know who to trust." And it mattered most of all if they were going to help the Morrigan take her temper out on Zac.

"No, it doesn't," she insisted. "You're thinking about this all wrong. Everyone is. They're trying to play catch up, but that's a game you can never win. We have to play our own game."

I stopped in the middle of the corridor and faced her. No one else was about at the moment, though I could hear the soft murmur of conversation coming from the kitchen a few doors along.

"Ceej, I'm really tired and I haven't had breakfast and I don't feel like playing guessing games. If you've got some better idea than everyone else, please share it. What is this masterful secret plan you're working on?"

She stepped closer and lowered her voice. "We have to get the cauldron back."

"What the hell for?" I snapped. "Geez, you say I'm obsessed. What's with you and the stupid cauldron? Even if we could get our hands on it—which we can't—what good would it do us?"

"It helped you before. You managed to pull three condensors out of it and almost defeat the Morrigan."

"That's because I was full to the brim with aether." I hadn't realised it at the time, but that had been one unexpected side benefit of the toads and diamonds curse. The aether that powered the curse had been enough to power the cauldron too. Without it all my wishing couldn't have produced a thing from the cauldron. "The Morrigan took it all with her when we banished her. The cauldron wouldn't respond to me any more. It's nothing but an ugly old pot without aether."

I tried not to sound bitter. For a while I'd thought I could work magic, and the sensation had been joyous. I still couldn't forget the dimming of that feeling, or how I'd felt something essential was being pulled from me when the Morrigan reclaimed my borrowed magic.

"The cauldron's been in bloody fairyland all this time," CJ said. "It produces the most amazing feasts. Cups of solid gold. Beautiful jewellery. Anything the Sidhe set their hearts on."

She sounded like she'd seen it in action. Had this Ariel guy shown her? "So?"

"So, it can work miracles there, because it's surrounded by aether. Some of that's got to seep in. Like recharging a battery. I bet it's all powered up now."

I sighed. "The crucial point in this admittedly appealing fantasy you're weaving being that it's *there*. And we're not."

"Then we need to change that," she said promptly, giving me a challenging look. "We'll have to go there and get it back. How hard can it be?"

"How hard—Are you *insane*? You're suggesting we waltz into the stronghold of Sidhe power and try to steal their most prized possession. And you think that won't be difficult? We have no weapons, no power, nothing to use against them. Do you think your Sidhe friend's going to help you steal the cauldron?"

"Would you rather keep waiting here for the next attack, doing nothing? Who's next? Mum? Dorian?"

I shook my head, fear a tight knot in my throat, constricting my breathing. Not them. Zac.

"It's only a matter of time before they win just by grinding us down," she persisted. "The cauldron's our best hope. Better than any of the weak artefacts they've got locked up in the vault. We can't keep doing nothing and just hope the Sidhe will somehow give up and go away."

No. I couldn't do nothing. But would he be safe in England? Everyone I cared about was in the firing line.

There was only one way I could think of that had even the slightest hope of keeping him safe, but I would have to be strong.

Chapter Nine

At lunchtime I wandered off to the kitchen to find some food. CJ had disappeared, taking the mirror with her, and I couldn't stand to be alone any more. Mum and Dena were there already, seated at the long table with their heads together, talking in low tones. Probably about Sona. I tried to listen in without appearing to, but I couldn't make out what they were saying. I wished I could tell them about the mirror and CJ's crazy plans, but they had enough on their plates already without adding another burden. I'd just have to deal with CJ myself.

While I sat there working my way through a plate of chicken salad, Dorian came in with Gretel. They helped themselves to food and sat down with Mum and Dena.

Dorian looked even worse than the last time I'd seen him. His face was drawn into deep lines, and his eyes were full of pain and ringed with shadows.

"You shouldn't be here, Dorian," said Mum. "We can handle things here. You should be at the hospice with Rebecca."

"She'd be the first to tell you you're wrong," he said. "We're running out of time, and you know it. If we don't act soon, there won't be anyone left *to* act."

Dena heaved a heavy sigh. "I don't see the point in rehashing this argument. I understand you're keen to do something. We all are. But it's never going to work without the cauldron."

I stared hard at my plate, hoping they'd forget I was here. This sounded interesting. What was never going to work without the cauldron? If someone finally had a plan CJ wouldn't have to continue her dangerous association with this Ariel guy.

Dorian leaned forward, waving his fork in the air for emphasis. "We have to at least try, Dena. What's the alternative? Sit here and wait while the Sidhe pick us off one by one? However hard we try, we can't seem to stop the leaks. For every one we plug, another five spring up. We'll be drowning in aether inside a month, and the Sidhe will have broken free for good."

"I'm sure we're not at that point yet," Dena said. "The walls could hold for months still."

"Months! If only I shared your optimism." Frustration warred with exhaustion on his face. "And in the meantime the rats keep slipping through the cracks. What use are walls if some of the prisoners can get through? 'At least not all the Sidhe can get free' is no kind of consolation. Even if only one of them can, that's one too many. And clearly one is enough to bring this organisation to its knees."

"I'm not saying we should do nothing." Dena's tone was tart, and I couldn't help wondering how much sleep she'd got last night. "But we can hardly renew four anchors with only three treasures."

I felt a stab of guilt. That damn cauldron had a lot to answer for.

Dorian slammed his hands down on the table top, and we all jumped. "Then what, Dena? You don't want to do nothing? Then what do we do? What in God's name is left that we haven't already tried?"

"Twice," said Mum, her tone exhausted. "All right then, say we agreed to renew the anchors. How do we get around the fact that we have no cauldron?"

"I've been thinking about that," said Dorian. "The reason the four treasures made such good anchors in the first place was because of the amount of aether imbued in them."

"And now they have none," Dena interjected, "so I don't see what use they'll be anyway, even if we were mad enough to bring them all here and dangle them like bait in front of the Sidhe's noses."

Dorian held up his hand for silence, like some kind of professor in a lecture hall. This was why I found it so difficult to warm to him—this assumption that everyone else should hush to hear his golden words of wisdom. If it bothered me, it must have annoyed the heck out of someone like Dena, who was his equal, but she fell silent and waited for him to speak.

"We're not creating the anchors from scratch," he said, when he had her full attention again. "So I don't think it will require much aether to strengthen them—at least not the other three. Our readings show us the main problem is here in Sydney, and that is where we should concentrate our efforts."

"What are you proposing?" Mum asked.

"I feel the aether in the vault may be enough to recharge the treasures for the other sites."

"And for here? What about Sydney?"

"We have three possible sources of major amounts of aether right here." He gave Mum a challenging look, but she seemed confused.

"What sources? What are you talking about?"

"I'm talking about Sergei. And Doug." He looked at Dena. "And now your granddaughter."

I nearly choked on my lettuce, and Mum looked my way, suddenly aware I was listening to every word. Dena looked ready to explode, but Mum touched her arm and indicated me with a nod of her head, and she reined in whatever she'd been about to say with a visible effort.

"If we could condense the aether out of them, we wouldn't *be* in this position," she hissed instead.

Mum pushed her chair back with a loud scraping noise. "I think we should take this conversation elsewhere. Excuse us, Gretel."

Dorian and Dena rose, too, and Gretel nodded as they filed out, slamming the door behind them.

"Whoa." I stared at Gretel. "That was pretty intense."

"Yep." She frowned down at her plate, as if she didn't want to talk about it, but I wasn't going to pass up an opportunity like this.

"Is Dorian right? Can the warders use the aether in them to strengthen the anchors?"

"How should I know?"

"It won't hurt them, will it?" Maybe that was why Dena was so upset at the thought.

"I shouldn't think so, but it's not as if anybody's tried whatever he's got in mind. Condensors haven't worked."

So maybe it *would* hurt. Perhaps a lot.

"Maybe he needs their blood."

She gave me a startled look. "Their *blood*? Why would you think that?"

"I heard they used blood in the original enchantments, when they set up the anchors. The blood of defectives."

"Who the hell told you that?"

Puck had, in fact, when he'd been imprisoned here last year. No one knew that I'd spoken to him—that in fact it was my fault he'd escaped—so I wasn't going to admit who'd told me. *Ask them what they do to defectives*, he'd said, implying it was something terrible. And I'd wondered whether he'd been making shit up just to scare me.

Only now that I saw the look on Gretel's face I could tell that he hadn't.

"We don't call them *defectives*." She practically spat the word. "That's a terrible insult. Have you been poking around in those books I left on your mother's desk?"

"No." At least that was something I could answer truthfully. Fortunately, she didn't ask about any other books.

"Well, I don't know who would tell you such a thing. It's not in any of the official histories, that's for sure." She shook her head, still giving me that suspicious look. "*Defectives*. Honestly, the things you come out with sometimes."

"Sorry. So it's not true? Nobody was sacrificed to build the anchors?" Her face went still, and my heart began to pound at that bleak look. "Oh, my God, it *is* true!"

She swallowed hard, and laid down her knife and fork. "It depends what you mean by sacrificed."

"Gretel!" This was no time for splitting hairs. "Sacrificed. Killed. Their blood taken to power the magic. Oh, no!" I gasped and covered my mouth with my hands. "He's going to kill Dad! And Sona!"

"Hey, no—wait!" She got up and came around the table to me. "Let's take a chill pill here. For heaven's sake, you're shaking." She pulled me to my feet and patted me awkwardly on the shoulder, as if she'd like to hug me but wasn't sure how I'd react. "He's not going to kill anyone. Calm down."

"You don't know that."

"Of course he isn't. Do you think Warder Bhutra would allow that? Do you think your *mother* would? Remember, we're not inventing the wheel here. The wheel's already been invented, this is just a little adjustment."

She offered me a glass of water and I took it, feeling my heart rate slowly return to normal. Gradually I stopped shaking, and managed to set the glass down without spilling anything.

"It's true that people … died as part of the original anchoring. And that they were non-latents. Kin of the original warders. Their blood had to be tied to the mages working the spell, you see. But no one was put to death against their will. They all volunteered for the role."

"Who would volunteer for such a thing?"

She sighed. "They all had their reasons. Two were a couple whose three children had all been killed by the Sidhe. Their whole family, wiped out. They felt they had nothing to live for. Another was dying already, probably of cancer, though they didn't know of such things at the time. But all of them shared a determination to lock the Sidhe out of our world for good, so they could do no more harm. They were all prepared to give their lives to make that happen."

I shook my head, still unable to comprehend how anyone could do it.

"You have to remember, this was a long time ago. People died of all sorts of things. Hardly anyone lived to old age. Death was a bigger part of life. Why do you think so many fairy tales are about stepmothers? Women and babies were dropping off the twig all the time. I guess this way they knew their deaths would mean something."

"Were the Sidhe that bad, that getting rid of them could be worth giving up your life for?"

"Well, not to everyone, maybe. It wasn't as if they were riding around killing people willy-nilly by the thousands. And some people loved them, even worshipped them as gods. But if you were one of the ones who suffered at their hands you probably would have felt it was pretty important."

"So the mages didn't suffer? None of them put up their hand to die to fuel the spell."

"It wasn't like that. It wasn't an 'us versus them' thing. Same as now, there just weren't that many people with the ability to become mages. Have you ever wondered how they picked the number seven? Seven warders?"

I shook my head. "It's some magical lucky number? I don't know."

"No. There were only seven mages powerful enough to work that spell in the whole world. But there were lots of people with just a touch of potential. They used to call it having the sight. And of course, there were millions more who were completely dead to magic. Regular people, like me and you. Well, not you, obviously. Your latency's like Dorian's. You could have been one of the seven in those days. But now we're all just regular people."

Except we weren't. There was definitely a hierarchy, based on their precious latency scores. Even if they didn't call them defective, they didn't treat people with low scores the same. Look at Gretel herself—she would have loved to be a seeker, but it wasn't allowed, because her latency score wasn't high enough. And CJ wouldn't even have been told about all this if we hadn't been attacked by the Sidhe. Her lack of latency meant she wasn't good enough even to know the warders existed.

Maybe she would have been one of the people sacrificed in ancient times. Her blood had the right DNA, it just wasn't potent enough for her to be a mage. Dorian had better not be thinking about sacrificing any "defectives".

I took my plate to the sink and threw the rest of my lunch in the rubbish. My appetite had fled, chased off by all this talk of sacrifices.

"So Dad and Sergei and Sona are safe?"

"Absolutely."

"But what happens to them if Dorian's idea succeeds?"

She frowned. "What do you mean?"

"I mean, if he manages to close the leaks for good. No more Sidhe threat, but also no more aether escaping. How are we ever going to fix them?"

Once all possibility of magic was removed from the world, how could we ever find a magical solution to their problems?

"Well, um, I guess we'll come up with something eventually. And it's not as if having the Sidhe threat hanging over us is *helping*, is it?"

No, but I couldn't help wondering whether more time would really make a difference. I was starting to think CJ was right: they needed a new approach, because the one they had wasn't working. I must have caught the cauldron bug from her, because its power was starting to look like a better and better option. Gretel might be prepared to close the way and let Dad and Sergei and Sona take their chances on someone eventually coming up with a cure for them, but I wasn't so keen on the idea. My dad wasn't going to be the sacrifice so that everyone else could be safe.

We didn't do sacrifices any more.

"Of course it's all theoretical at the moment anyway," Gretel said. "We can talk about closing the leaks until the cows come home, but that doesn't make it happen. Frankly, I'd be surprised if even Dorian can manage it without the cauldron."

"Yeah. Right."

Even more reason to get the damn thing back, then. We could use its power to help the Sidhe's victims, and then turn it on the Sidhe themselves. Poetic justice.

I went to find CJ.

School that week felt weird without Sona. It was funny how quickly some people wormed their way into your life and your heart. We'd only moved to Sydney in September last year, so I'd known her less than six months, but already we were closer than I'd been to the friends I'd had for three years in Townsville.

And that went double for Zac. He sat next to me on the bus now Sona was gone, and held my hand. That should have helped, but knowing what I had to do, it only made it worse. Soon he'd be gone too. But I kept putting it off, clinging to that hand as if I were drowning and he was the only thing keeping me afloat. All week I stored memories of him: the way that adorable dimple peeped out when he smiled, the feel of his big hand wrapped around mine, the tenderness in his voice. I treasured up little snapshots of our life together to try to sustain me through what was coming. Zac cheering his team on from the sidelines during sport. Zac carrying my bag for me, one arm slung over my shoulder. Zac smiling, Zac laughing, Zac kissing me under the shade of the trees in the playground, the smell of the lemon-scented gum forever linked with the feel of his mouth warm on mine.

"What do you want to do on the weekend?" he asked on Friday. "Some of the guys are going to the movies. Want to go with them?"

I'd put it off all week. I couldn't put it off any more, not if I was serious about protecting him.

"When are your mum and the kids leaving?"

His dad was gone already. The guy who'd had the job before him had died unexpectedly, and someone had to fill the gap immediately. The minute Zac's dad decided to take the job they had him on a plane to London, and it was left to Zac's mum to pack up their old life and organise the move.

"They're heading over next week to check out places to live, and Mum wants to find a good school for Gemma and Ryan, but she'll be back to finish packing up and selling the house. Why?"

"I think you should go with them."

He looked like I'd just punched him in the gut. In the sudden silence I heard him swallow, and watched his Adam's apple bob up and down as he fought to hide his reaction.

"To help with the house-hunting, you mean?" he said at last.

I took a deep breath. Now or never.

"When will you ever get an opportunity like this again? To live in another country, not just be a tourist. You should go with them. Move over there."

"You want me to leave you?"

No, of course I don't! I love you. The pain in his eyes was killing me. But I couldn't take it back, couldn't tell him what this was really about, or he'd refuse to go. He'd want to stay and tough it out, and then he too would go down, victim of another Sidhe attack. There was no standing against the Morrigan. I remembered her in the Art Gallery, crows swirling around her in a magical tempest, lightning sparking from her fingertips. Even locked on the other side of the wall, she somehow had the power to reach into our world and wreak havoc. She'd taken nearly everyone I loved already. I couldn't let Zac go down, too.

"It's a great opportunity," I repeated, like a broken record.

"But I thought ..." He stopped and tried again. His face had gone very pale. "You begged me to stay. You said you *needed* me to stay."

No, I need you to be safe.

"I know, and I feel really bad about putting that on you. I shouldn't have done that. Your family needs you too, you know. Gemma and Ryan would miss you terribly if you stayed behind."

He shook his head. "They'll get over it. I've made my decision."

Oh, God. How could I persuade him to go when every fibre of my being was aching for him to stay? I'd never been a great actress, but I was going to have to learn fast.

"So unmake it." I shrugged, as if this were no big deal.

He turned away in an explosive movement. "I can't believe you. Last week you were crying all over me, begging me to stay, and now you're telling me to go? What is your issue?"

"No issue. It just caught me by surprise, that's all. Now I've had time to think about it, I've changed my mind."

"You've changed your mind." His voice was heavy with disbelief.

"Yes." I took a deep breath. I *had* to persuade him. "It might be a good idea for us to take a break. This is perfect timing."

"Take a break?"

The hurt on his face made me want to cry, but I forged on. "Yeah, you know. Things are pretty intense with my family right now. I just think I need to focus on that, without so many … distractions."

A flash of anger sparked his dark eyes. "Distractions? Is that what this is? I'm a *distraction* to you?"

"I just don't think I can be in a relationship right now." I had to look at the bridge of his nose. I couldn't bear to see the look in his eyes. "It's probably best if we just call it quits. That way we're both free agents and you can go to England. No hard feelings."

He was breathing hard, angry now. Or maybe it was shock. I don't know; I was concentrating too hard on not crying. This was sheer torture, the hardest thing I'd ever done. Worse even than standing up to the Morrigan.

"You want to call it off? You want to be 'free'? Why? Have you found somebody else?"

I didn't answer. I couldn't speak, but he drew his own conclusions from my silence.

"That's it, isn't it? Who is it? Someone from the warders, I suppose. Is it that Simon guy?" He glared down at me and something inside me shrivelled up and died. "Well, good luck to him. He'll need it."

He stormed off. I closed my eyes and let the slow tears well.

Chapter Ten

I stared at the bust of Hans Christian Andersen and thought nasty thoughts. Lucky for him he was already dead or I'd have killed him, the miserable bastard. Why had he written such depressing fairy tales? Him and his stupid red shoes.

CJ and I were on Observatory Hill. The bust stood on its plinth outside the fence that surrounded the grounds of the Observatory proper. The Observatory was an old sandstone building with a dome of light green copper at either end, and a tower in the middle that supported a golden ball on a stick that looked very much like an upside-down Chuppa Chup. The golden ball had been here for years, and used to be raised up on its stick every day just before one o'clock in the afternoon. In the days when Sydney was a tiny colony several months' voyage away from civilisation, it was important for navigation to know the exact time. At one o'clock precisely the ball had dropped, allowing the ships floating in the harbour below to set their chronometers accordingly before attempting the long and perilous journey back to the northern hemisphere.

The bust of Hans was much newer, and had been donated by the Danish royal family only a few years ago. It always seemed odd to me to find a statue of a Danish storyteller in the heart of historic Sydney, but it was oddly fitting, considering the very real magical history of this particular part of it. Maybe the Danes had had a sixth sense that told them this would be a good spot for old Hans to sit, looking out across the rooftops toward the Harbour Bridge.

Kyle was on duty today, sitting on the park bench with his iPad. He could have been a tourist, or some young guy on his lunch break, and no one took the slightest notice of him. They might have been surprised if they could have seen the app he was using, but most of them were admiring the view, or tramping around the Observatory taking photos. This was a popular spot for wedding photos, with the Harbour Bridge lurking so photogenically in the background, and there was already one wedding party here, despite the early hour.

I wandered over to the bench. "Everything quiet up here?"

He shrugged. "There's still a leak. You can probably smell it—over there." He jerked his head toward the fence around the Observatory. "Simon said you were a powerful latent."

We wandered over to the fence.

"So where's this leak?" CJ asked.

I sniffed the air, and got a whiff of burnt toffee. "Right here."

That was the unmistakeable scent of aether, the raw material of magic. It was all supposed to be penned in with the Sidhe in their prison, safely walled off from our mundane world. But according to that smell, there was definitely something leaking through, however small.

Her expression soured. "Guess I'll just have to trust you on that one. Can't smell anything with my pathetic latency."

"Don't be such a princess." I wasn't in the mood for her sulking. My head pounded from all the crying I'd done last night and I just wanted to curl up in a ball and wait for the world to go away. I couldn't see why everyone made such a big deal over latency scores when we were all hoping to God that "latency" was as far as it ever got. If the aether stayed where it was supposed to be, latency scores, however impressive, were only numbers on a page. If we got to the point where they actually meant something, the Sidhe would be free and we'd all be in deep shit. Whether or not I could do magic would be the furthest thing from anyone's mind then.

"So you've got no latent magical powers," I snapped. "Big deal. The only thing they're good for is being able to smell aether. You can't actually *do* anything with them. I'd trade mine any time for all the advantages *you* have."

"Such as?"

The trouble with CJ was that she was so used to being admired she hardly even noticed her natural assets. They were just part of the package she took for granted. She only wanted things that other people had that she didn't, like Sona's luscious hair, or my useless latency scores.

"Gee, I don't know. How about being taller than a flipping five-year-old? That'd be a nice start."

"What's up your nose this morning?" For the first time she took a good look at me, and her tone changed from accusing to concerned. "Are you all right? Your eyes are all red. Have you been crying?"

I could have said my allergies were playing up, but what the hell. I was sick of putting on a brave face. "I broke up with Zac yesterday."

"What?" She looked genuinely shocked. "But you were such a great couple. He was a big fat nerd, and so are you. What happened?"

I shrugged. "His family's moving overseas. There didn't seem much point dragging it out." I didn't tell her I'd done it to save him from the Morrigan. Talking about it made it feel too real.

"Bummer." She pulled me into a hug. I put my arms around her waist and rested my head against her shoulder, breathing in the familiar scent of her shampoo. "Are you okay?"

"Not really." Tears stung my eyes, and her arms tightened around me.

"Stupid boys." She dropped a kiss on the top of my head. "We'd be better off without them."

"I just miss him so much." I shoved her away and scrubbed at my face. "You really shouldn't be nice to me. It only makes me want to cry more."

"Then let's get back to work."

She grabbed my hand and dragged me behind her around the fence line. At least I still had CJ. She could be annoying as hell sometimes, but when push came to shove I knew I could always count on her to be there for me.

She stopped when we'd gone far enough that we could no longer see Kyle on his bench.

"What about here? Still the same level?"

I sniffed cautiously. "No. There's some—I can still make it out—but it's not as strong."

"Shame," she said. "I'd really rather not open a gateway right under a bloody seeker's nose."

She made it sound so easy, as if she could just press a button and magic a gateway into existence.

"How are we going to do that, anyway? Just because there's aether leaking doesn't mean we can use it to get through. What did Ariel say?"

"He says he can open a gate if we find 'an optimum place'."

"Really? If it's so easy to open a gate how come they're all still trapped on the other side?"

"How should I know?"

"Well, what do you guys talk about all the time?"

"Oh, you know." She waved her hand airily. "Just stuff. Trust me, Vi, I know what I'm doing. If I start interrogating him, he's going to get suspicious, isn't he?"

I supposed she had a point there. "Why does he want you to come to fairyland? He must have said that, at least."

"He just wants to meet me. He says he's not powerful enough to get out, so I have to come to him." She glanced across at Kyle. "We should probably go at night, so the warders don't see us opening the gate."

"They monitor this place around the clock, you know. It's not as if the Sidhe have signed a contract to only pop out in daylight hours."

"Hmmm." Her face fell. "That's a shame. I guess at least in daylight there's other people around."

"Especially on the weekend," I said. "You think it's busy now, you should see it this afternoon. More brides than you can poke a stick at. People everywhere." I looked up at the deep cloudless blue above me. "Especially on a day like today."

"We'll need to take food and drink."

"Good thinking." Lots of the old stories mentioned the danger of accepting food or drink from the fairies. You could get turned into an animal, or sleep away a hundred years. Their gifts were not to be trusted. "What else?"

It felt more than a little surreal to be planning an invasion of fairyland. Surrounded by magic, how were we going to protect ourselves, much less force the Sidhe to give up the cauldron? We were mad to even consider it.

"Weapons."

I stared. "What?"

"Oh, come on. How else are we going to stand up to them? There's two of us, and who knows how many of them?"

"But …" I guess I'd been thinking of something a little more covert. Standing up to the might of the Sidhe was a very long way from the top of my Things I'd Like To Do One Day list. "We don't have any weapons. Unless you count my old baseball bat."

"Sure we do. Headquarters is full of them. Condensors, and all their other tricky little gadgets."

"Condensors won't work." Geez, didn't she know anything? "They suck the aether out of things and collapse it back into the Sidhe world, like a magic vacuum cleaner. If we're already *in* the Sidhe world, what's going to happen? A big fat lot of nothing."

She waved her hand in an impatient gesture. CJ was a big-picture thinker, not a details person. "Well, I'm sure we can find something useful. If not, there's always guns."

"*Guns?* Are you nuts? You've never even fired a gun. Do you even know how to load one? Or aim it?"

"It can't be that hard," she said. "In America even little kids do it. You just point and shoot."

"Yeah, most likely you'll shoot *me.*"

She shrugged. "Well, the Sidhe don't know that, do they? I can just threaten them with it."

"Quite apart from the fact that we don't *have* any guns … or are you planning to steal them from one of the seekers?"

She said nothing, just gave me that look—the one that said *So? You wanna make something of it?*

I groaned. This was getting out of hand. "Look, let's just forget it, okay? This is never going to work. Maybe we should talk to Mum about it. If the warders sent a group in they might actually have a chance of succeeding."

"No way." She gripped my arm hard and whirled me to face her. "Promise me you won't tell Mum."

"Why not? It makes more sense."

"Use your head, Vi! There's a traitor in the warders and *we don't know who it is.*"

"But it's not Mum!"

"No, of course not. But as soon as she tells someone, the plan's in danger. If the traitor finds out, we could lose our last chance to save Dad. Promise me, Vi!"

"Okay, okay." I dragged my arm out of her grip, rubbing at the sore spot where the marks of her fingers showed. I'd probably have a bruise there. "I promise."

***

When we got back to headquarters the atmosphere was tense. I went looking for Gretel, after promising CJ yet again that I wouldn't say anything to Mum about a trip inside the gilded cage. I couldn't find Gretel, but I did find Ronnie in the monitor room again. She seemed to be living there lately. Her desk was scattered with the remains of at least two meals, and she looked as though it had been a while since she'd slept. Or even brushed her hair.

The only sounds in the big room were the gentle hum of the machines and the tapping of keyboards. It took me a minute to realise it, but walking across the large space started to feel creepy once I noticed that not a single person there was speaking. And there were at least twenty, maybe thirty of them. It wasn't natural.

I stopped by Ronnie's desk and dropped my voice to a whisper. It felt like talking in church. Any minute now someone was going to yell at me to be more respectful and tell me to open my hymn book to page 352.

"Why's everyone so quiet? Has something happened?"

The big screen showed the familiar map of the world. The rest of the world was still clear. Only Australia seemed infested by leaking aether.

"The warders have been talking." Her voice was also low, and I drew even closer. "Arguing, actually. Everyone's walking on eggshells. No one wants to set them off again."

"What are they arguing about?"

"Same old same old. Renewing the anchors."

"Huh. I thought Dorian had already won that battle."

"Well, he has now, but Warder Bhutra is *not* happy about it. And she's not the only one." She looked over her shoulder, making me feel like we were two conspirators plotting together.

"There's quite a few of us that agree with her. It's a crazy idea."

I pushed a half-eaten sandwich out of the way and perched on the edge of her desk. "Why? Are you afraid we'll never find a way to help Dad and Sona and Sergei once they renew the anchors?"

She shook her head. "I don't think it will have any effect on that. But to strengthen the anchors they'll have to bring all the treasures back to Australia, where they'll be in easy reach of any Sidhe wandering outside the walls. Why do you think the Founders scattered them across the globe in the first place? They were kept separate for a reason, you know."

"Do you think the Sidhe will come after them?"

"Who knows what the Sidhe will do? But if they find out what we're doing, and manage to take back the other three treasures, we're screwed. And they already have the cauldron."

"Don't remind me."

"Warder Bhutra thinks we could have months yet, before they're able to do more than sneak an occasional Sidhe through the barrier. Surely we could work something out in time, something that wouldn't go against everything we've been taught. Protect the treasures at all costs—that's our mission."

"I thought your mission was keeping the Sidhe out of our world."

"They go hand in hand."

"What if you're all wrong, and closing the leaks means we can never find a cure for Dad and Sona?" The sooner we got that damn cauldron back the better.

She blew out an explosive breath. Several people working nearby looked up. "We have aether here in the vault. I'm sure someone will come up with something eventually. We just need more time."

They'd had plenty of time. CJ was right. We were Dad's only hope. "So they decided to go ahead with Dorian's plan?"

"Yep. The vote was close, three to two. And now Warder Bhutra and Warder Davidson aren't speaking to the other three."

"They were the two who voted against?" My own mother had voted to condemn Dad to life as a polar bear. That stung.

"Uh-huh."

"So what happens now?"

"Now we wait while the sword and the stone are retrieved from their hiding places. Once they arrive, someone will release the spear."

I nodded. The spear was here in Sydney, hidden somewhere in St Mary's Cathedral. I'd looked for it that day I'd been running for sanctuary with the cauldron, with the Morrigan and her forces on my tail, but I hadn't been able to find it. I guess that was the point, though. No use hiding something so that anyone walking in off the street would be able to spot it.

"Who's going to get the sword and the stone?" It would be just our luck if our mysterious traitor got their hands on the other treasures too. "It'll have to be someone we can trust."

"Of course." She gave me a quizzical look. "Don't worry, the warders are on top of that, at least. Warder Jonasson and Simon will retrieve the sword, and Warder Davidson and his sister have already left for Ireland. They're going for the stone."

I swallowed. "Kerrie? Bryan's taking Kerrie to get the stone?"

"Is that a problem? She's one of our best seekers."

I hadn't mentioned my suspicions of Kerrie to anyone but

CJ. Maybe I was wrong, and I'd just look like a paranoid idiot, but …

I took a deep breath. "She was in France last year."

Ronnie knew immediately what I was referring to. "But not in Paris."

"So she said."

Ronnie's eyebrows nearly disappeared into her hair. "You're accusing *her*? Sister of a warder, the woman who got hit with the Snow White curse?"

"I know it seems unlikely—"

"Unlikely! You're talking crazy talk."

"Ron, someone did it. It's got to be someone fairly high up in the organisation, to even know where and how the cauldron was hidden. They don't tell stuff like that to just anyone, do they?"

"Not even the seekers," she said.

"Right. But her brother's a warder, so it fits, see? Unless you think one of the warders did it. And she was so weird when I asked her about her trip, as if she was repeating a story she'd been told. She flew into Marseilles on Friday night, stayed there until Sunday, then she hired a car and went touring. She *says* she went to Orange and Lascaux and a couple of other places, but she could have gone to Paris, couldn't she?"

"Except that she was truth-tested, just like everyone else, and she wasn't lying."

God, this was so frustrating. "But someone must have been, mustn't they? The cauldron didn't wander round the bloody Louvre on its own."

Ronnie sighed. "You really have a bee in your bonnet about

this, don't you? I thought you liked Kerrie. You seemed so thrilled when she woke up."

"I was." Well, kind of. "I just don't trust her."

"Why not? What possible motive could she have?"

"I don't know." That was where my theory fell down, of course. I couldn't see a reason for anyone with half a brain to aid the Sidhe against humanity. "But she had the knowledge and the opportunity."

"So did a couple of the Paris staff, but you're not accusing them. It's not illegal to have a holiday, you know."

I folded my arms, feeling like a little kid throwing a tantrum, and just as powerless. "There was just something funny about the way she practically recited her itinerary. All I did was ask about her holiday. It was almost like she was trying to prove she had an alibi."

Ronnie shrugged. "Well, I could call up her truth test for you if you like. And the ones for the Paris staff too. Maybe that will convince you she's clear."

"Just Kerrie's."

She tapped a series of commands on her keyboard. "You're relentless, aren't you? I hope you never decide *I've* done something wrong."

A document appeared on her screen, and she rolled her chair a little to the side so I could see better. It was short, and I skimmed quickly through it.

"See?" said Ronnie. "Orange and Nimes on Sunday, she's even given the places she stayed Sunday and Monday nights— and we checked them out, they have a record of her being there—then Lascaux and La Roque St Christophe on Mondaaaay … hang on."

She frowned at the screen and sat up straighter in her chair. "What? What's wrong?"

She opened a web browser and began typing into a search engine. "Maybe things have changed in the last few years …"

A website on Lascaux opened, showing a party of tourists exclaiming over cave paintings of bison and other animals. Ronnie's eyes flicked over the accompanying text, and her shoulders drooped.

"Bloody hell." She looked up at me, and I could tell she now believed me. "Nope, nothing's changed. Gretel and I went to France a few years ago. We hired a car and drove ourselves around—had a really packed schedule, there was so much we wanted to see and we only had two weeks. I'd been looking forward to seeing the cave paintings at Lascaux, but we got there on a Monday and we didn't have time to hang around until the next day, so we missed out. Lots of things in France close on Mondays. And Lascaux is one of them."

Funny how I didn't get any warm glow out of being right.

"So Kerrie couldn't have been there."

"Exactly. I don't know how she fooled the truth test, but she's lying. And if she wasn't at Lascaux, where was she?"

"I think we both know the answer to that."

She nodded. "We need to talk to your mother straight away."

Chapter Eleven

Mum couldn't get hold of Bryan, since he was still in the air, so she called ahead to the Irish branch. I heard there was a difficult scene at the airport when they had to explain to Bryan why they were taking his sister into custody, especially since he knew she'd passed the truth test. Mum got an irate phone call in the middle of the night, and it took her a long time to calm him down enough to explain what we'd discovered.

For a while there, I worried that Bryan was in on it too, though Mum refused to even consider the possibility. Perhaps he'd take the stone and disappear. Then we'd be down two of the four treasures. Dorian would have a snowball's chance in hell of reinforcing any anchors then. That was something, at least.

But two days later Bryan arrived back in Sydney, having stayed in Ireland barely long enough to sleep before facing the gruelling flight home. Kerrie was on a different flight, in the custody of two dour-faced Irishmen. Bryan had exploded all over again when Mum suggested we couldn't risk having Kerrie on the same flight as the stone, but he'd eventually agreed to the separation.

He was crankier than Sergei when he returned, and that was saying something: ogres' bad tempers are legendary. But at least he had the stone safe and sound, though it didn't look like much when he produced it. It really was just a hunk of ordinary old stone—no engravings, no precious jewels inlaid, nothing. But the other warders were satisfied it was the real thing, so I could stop worrying about another switcheroo, at least.

It sat now on the coffee table in our guest suite's lounge area, with the warders seated around it. Mum and Dorian were on one lounge, and Dena and Bryan took the one opposite, neatly demonstrating the division amongst the warders. Frida was still off with Simon picking up the sword. I cast a sideways glance at Ronnie. She looked as uncomfortable as I felt to be here, as if it was our fault for accusing Kerrie, rather than hers for turning traitor in the first place.

"There must have been a flaw with her truth-test," Dorian said. "We'll have to run another one."

Bryan looked pained. They'd all seen the transcripts of the first one, and heard Ronnie's explanations. I said nothing, quite happy for Ronnie to take the brunt of Bryan's anguished expression.

"I just don't understand," he kept saying. "Why would she? It's not like her at all. It doesn't make sense."

But he couldn't argue with the facts.

"We need to get to the bottom of this," said Mum. "Had she been having any trouble at work? Did she seem to be acting strangely, or have changed in any way recently?"

"No, no." Bryan shook his head impatiently. "I'm telling you, she's the same person she's always been. There was nothing like that."

"Any problems in her personal life?"

"You think she'd turn against us because she broke up with her *boyfriend*? Is that what you think of her?" Bryan's face was turning redder by the moment. "No wonder you're so ready to believe the worst of her. She's as loyal as you or I. There must be some other explanation."

"If there is, we'll find it," Dorian assured him. "But I think you must prepare yourself for the worst."

Bryan's face set in mutinous lines. "This is utter shite."

"The stone will tell." Dorian looked at Mum, and she nodded. "Ronnie, if you would?"

Ronnie nodded and went to the door of the suite. When she came back she had Kyle and Kerrie with her. Kerrie wasn't wearing handcuffs or anything that said "prisoner", but Kyle stuck to her like glue. If she sneezed, he was going to wear it, and she had no chance of getting away.

Not that she seemed to want to. She marched in, head held high. Her face was pale except for two bright spots of colour on her cheeks, and she looked more like Snow White than ever with her dark hair down around her face. All she needed was the blue and yellow dress—and maybe a woodland creature perched on her shoulder—and the resemblance would be perfect.

Dorian gestured her to a lone chair by the stone. She took it, and Kyle moved into position behind her, looming over her petite form. Ronnie resumed her seat next to me.

"What are they going to do?" I whispered to her.

"Just watch," she whispered back.

Kerrie's eyes flicked to her brother, then settled on Dorian's face. "I haven't done anything wrong."

"That's what we need to settle today," said Mum. Her face was hard, a look that CJ and I didn't often see. "We are going to use the stone."

"To do what? I'm no king. The stone won't sing for me."

"But you are descended from one," Dorian said. I figured he wouldn't let Mum run the show for long. He did love the sound of his own voice. "Not in a direct line, of course, but your blood is close enough to work the magic of the stone."

She looked frankly disbelieving, and I had to admit I shared her scepticism. I leaned closer to Ronnie. "I thought magic didn't work any more?"

She barely moved her lips as she spoke, trying not to draw the attention of the warders. "The stone spent the night in the vault, soaking in aether. Hopefully it will be enough for this."

"The stone does more than cry out in the presence of the rightful king of Ireland," Dorian continued. "It can also tell the future for the king and his heirs, though like all such foretellings, the fortunes it gives are so cryptic as to be useless for any practical purpose. What is not so well known is that the stone can be used to see the past."

"It's not something that comes in handy too often, as you can imagine," said Mum. She glanced across at me, and I gathered that this was mainly for my benefit. "Most people already know their own past, and this ability isn't as glamorous or useful as being able to predict the future, however unclear those predictions may be. But in this case …"

"In this case, it will prove that I'm telling the truth, and then you can all stop wasting time accusing me and go and find the real culprit," said Kerrie.

"Then place your hand on the stone and we'll begin," said Dorian.

She slapped her hand down in a defiant gesture. Dorian placed his more gently over the top and began to chant in another language. It had a lilting, almost melodic quality. I looked at Ronnie.

"Old Irish," she whispered.

Dorian was soon finished, and I waited eagerly for something to happen. Nothing did. Dorian and the other warders stared at the stone in silence. Maybe it was speaking into their minds? Bummer. I'd been hoping for something a little more exciting.

I turned to Ronnie again, but she nudged me and jerked her head at the stone. When I looked back a cloud was forming above it, writhing like a storm at sea. Now *that* was more like it.

Dorian spoke again and a picture appeared in the cloud, insubstantial as mist, but clear enough to see. It was like watching a movie where the camera was weaving its way through a crowd of people. In the background a strange glass pyramid hulked above the people.

"What's that?" I whispered.

"The Louvre, in Paris." Ronnie's voice sounded shocked, even though this was what we'd expected. "We're seeing Kerrie's memories."

I looked at Kerrie herself. Her face was so white I thought she might pass out, her eyes wide with shock.

"No!" she said. "How are you doing this? That's not my memory! I've never been to Paris."

Dorian didn't answer, and she became more agitated as the strange movie continued. We followed the crowds inside, and I wished she had stopped to look around, because the glimpses I caught looked fascinating, but she moved like a woman on a mission. I saw her hand reach out to a door with something printed on it in French in big insistent letters.

"Staff only," Ronnie whispered.

We moved down a service corridor with her until she came to what looked like a smaller version of the monitor room here, full of screens and computer consoles and boards full of switches. One of the two men there looked up in surprise as she entered and her hand came out again. Something shot from the end of it like a bolt of blue lightning, and I jumped.

"What was that?"

"Aether." Mum's voice was hard enough to cut diamonds.

The man seemed unhurt. He turned back to his screens and continued what he'd been doing as if Kerrie wasn't there. The other man received the same blue bolt, and they chatted to each other in French as if they were alone, ignoring the switches that Kerrie was flicking and the alarms that began to blink on their console. Before she left the room I noticed several of the screens had gone dark.

"Make him stop, Bryan!" Kerrie begged. "He's making this all up!"

She tried to pull her hand away from the stone, but Kyle swooped on her and held her arms tight. Bryan didn't look at her, his face a mask of horror as he watched her memory continue to play out.

We moved back out into the public spaces, and threaded a winding path through galleries and up and down staircases. I'd heard the Louvre was big, but I'd never realised just how big.

How had Kerrie found her way? She seemed to know exactly where she was going.

At last we arrived in a smaller room, tucked a little out of the way. Obviously none of the big crowd-pleasing exhibits were in here, because there were only a handful of people strolling among the glass cabinets. I thought I recognised a couple of the items on display: they looked like some of the Greek treasures that had toured Australia last year. We'd seen them on our ill-fated excursion to the Art Gallery.

The people began to file out of the room as if at some silent command. More magic? Once they were all gone a blue flash lit the room briefly, and something shimmered in the large archway that led back to the rest of the gallery. The view through it was blurry, as if we saw the next room through a curtain of water, but Kerrie turned away from it before any of us could get a proper look at what she'd done. But no one else came in, so it seemed like some kind of force field. Maybe from the other side the opening had disappeared?

Where was she getting all this aether from? And how was she using it to perform magic? She wasn't even a warder, just a seeker. She must have had some latent abilities, or she couldn't have become a seeker, but I was quite certain that seekers weren't trained in the use of magic. Why would they be? Casting spells was hardly part of the job description.

A new display case came into view. It was a little dizzying to see everything through Kerrie's eyes, especially when she moved her head suddenly. But now she focused on the case in front of her, and the familiar squat shape of the pot inside it. That was it, in all its ugly glory. The cauldron of the Dagda.

She moved her hand over the discreet lock at the bottom of the case and a small blue light flared. The case popped open, with no more effort than that. She reached in and removed the cauldron. No alarms sounded. Nothing happened when she crossed the room and opened another case either. From that one she removed a jug, and put the cauldron in its place. Once her hands left it, the familiar outline of the cauldron blurred, and it took on the shape of the jug.

And of course, once the jug was put into the cauldron's case, it assumed the shape of the cauldron. Both doors swung shut with an audible click and Kerrie stepped back. The room looked just as it had before, the cauldron in its case in the centre of the room, and the jug part of the Spartan display in the other case. Only we knew of the switch that had taken place.

The scene froze there.

Dorian sighed. "Well, that seems fairly conclusive. I'm sorry, Bryan."

"No!" Kerrie's head whipped around to stare imploringly at her brother. "Don't believe him! He's trying to frame me."

"Bryan knows a little more than you about how the stone works," Mum said, when Bryan didn't—or couldn't—reply. "These are genuine memories, pulled straight from your head."

"How could you?" Bryan burst out. "My own sister, working with the Sidhe."

"I'm not! Bryan, I swear to you. That's not my memory." She was weeping, and snot trickled onto her top lip. She wiped it with her free hand. Dorian still had her other trapped under his on the stone. Kyle's heavy grip held her in place, but she no longer struggled to be free.

Dorian leaned forward, an avid gleam in his eye. He looked more alive than I'd seen him for weeks. "How did you accomplish this? Who gave you these spells? Where did you get the power?"

Power. I remembered what that felt like. The strange wrench inside, the tickle of burnt toffee in your nose making you want to sneeze. My fingers twitched involuntarily at the memory of the origami bird changing in my hand and taking flight, no longer paper but a creature of flesh and blood.

Or as much a creature of flesh and blood as any of the Morrigan's familiars were. Real crows and ravens couldn't coalesce out of mist they way they could. And it turned out I hadn't been doing magic of my own, as I'd thought. She'd tricked me, "gifting" me the little origami bird already booby-trapped with her spell, to be transformed when I focused enough aether on it later. Fairy gifts were always dodgy like that. Nothing good ever came of accepting one—not that I'd accepted it of my own free will, of course. That had been her doing too, compelling me to take the thing, and once taken, to forget I had it.

But still, I'd touched that power, and it had felt good. To be able to do what Kerrie had done, without even chanting a spell— to be able to work magic merely by wanting something done— was something people had always dreamed of. Better even than winning the lottery.

Kerrie sobbed. "I didn't have any power! That never happened, I swear."

Maybe not such a dream come true when you got caught. What would happen to her now? None of the warders' faces showed any understanding, or hope of forgiveness.

"Don't lie," Dena snapped. "We all saw what you did. Continuing to deny it doesn't help you."

"But it's true! I don't remember any of that. I swear I was never in Paris—I was in Nimes. I remember it—it had an amphitheatre like the Colosseum in Rome, there were broken pillars and statues. My boyfriend took a photo of me on the steps. I can show you! And we went to Orange and Lascaux."

"That's right," said Mum. "You went to Lascaux to see the cave paintings."

"Yes! They were amazing. I remember it all."

"Lascaux is closed on Mondays. You were never there."

"Then why do I remember going there? I can see those paintings in my mind, clear as day. I never went near Paris, or the Louvre. Someone's planted that in my brain, it's not true." She glared at Dorian with deep suspicion.

Whoa. Was that even possible? Could magic plant a false memory in your brain that you didn't even know was there? But who had the power to do that? Not Dorian, that was for sure. And why would they? To make Kerrie a scapegoat? But in that case, someone else still must have done what Kerrie's memories showed her doing. *Someone* had switched the cauldron. It all seemed a bit convoluted. Zac was pretty fond of quoting Occam's Razor: the simplest explanation was usually correct.

But Mum was looking thoughtfully at Dorian. "Perhaps Kerrie's on to something."

He looked sceptical. "You think someone's planted false memories of Paris in her mind to be discovered later?"

"No. I'm fairly certain the Paris memories are true."

Kerrie cried out in frustration, but Mum ignored her.

"I doubt we were ever meant to discover them." Mum continued. "It's far more likely the holiday memories of Lascaux and Nimes are the false ones, planted so that she could truthfully deny any wrongdoing."

"And therefore remain a trusted member of our organisation," Dorian finished. The warders all contemplated Kerrie now, speculation in their gazes. "The question then becomes, is she a cat's paw who didn't know what she was doing, or is she a willing accomplice in this deception?"

I wished they would stop talking about her as if she wasn't there. She'd stopped crying, but she was shaking so hard I could see it from here. If she had been duped by some Sidhe who'd screwed with her brain, we should be trying to help her, not treating her like a criminal. Guiltily I thought of the little origami bird again. It could happen to anyone.

"Let's find out," said Mum. "Go back through her memories."

Dorian said something else in Old Irish and a new picture began to form in the air above the stone. It showed dancing, and lots of smiling people. It looked like a wedding reception, and sure enough, a bride and groom danced into view in a moment, she with her veiled head nestled in the crook of his shoulder. This must be the wedding she'd gone to France to attend.

"Further back," said Mum.

I'd have to find out how this thing worked. Every time Dorian spoke, the picture changed, but of course I couldn't understand what he was saying. Was he asking the stone questions, or treating it like a DVD player, telling it to scroll forward and back in time? And what else could the stone do?

Maybe there was some other trick no one had thought to mention that might help CJ and me in our quest to get the cauldron back. God knew we needed all the help we could get.

Dorian spent some time flitting through Kerrie's memories. He seemed to be able to hit the highlights, so there was no cleaning teeth or eating breakfast-type stuff. Though her boyfriend appeared, there was no up-close-and-personal stuff either, which was probably a relief to everyone in the room.

Nothing else that she did in France seemed relevant. There was certainly no sightseeing. The day after the wedding she and her boyfriend drove straight to Paris and took a room. I didn't know what the boyfriend did, but he didn't feature in any further memories until they boarded the plane home back in Marseilles again. As for Kerrie, there were no meetings with obviously shady characters, or mysterious self-destructing messages telling her how to infiltrate the Louvre's security. For all we could see, she planned and executed it all on her own.

"Further." Mum turned her frustrated gaze on Kerrie. "What happened last time you were in Sydney?"

"I haven't been back to Sydney, apart from this trip, since I woke up," she replied.

"Let's see that."

Dorian nodded. The picture in the mists went dark, and the next thing we saw a close-up of Simon's face. Behind him at an odd angle we could see a door and another person. I tipped my head to one side and realised the angle was because she was lying in a bed, and the person in the background was me. We really had come right to the moment she opened her eyes after her long enchanted sleep.

"She's awake!" Simon's voice held all the awe and excitement I remembered.

Kerrie asked for water and he rushed from the room. In a moment Bryan burst in, his face alight with joy. Such a sad contrast to the expression it held now. More people crowded in behind him, their voices raised in an excited babble. I couldn't help smiling; their happiness was infectious. It had been an amazing moment.

It was kind of strange reliving it from someone else's perspective. Kerrie focused mainly on her brother's face, and the rest of the room faded into the background. I'd been more concerned with Simon's reaction at the time and I hadn't noticed the same details she had. But there was nothing in her memories to enlighten us.

"Further," Mum said impatiently. "Before she woke."

I leaned forward eagerly. Would we finally get to see who had put Kerrie into her magical sleep?

But before she woke there was only blackness and roiling mist. Dorian spoke sharply, but the next scene the stone showed us was in an airport, not in a small clearing in the forest.

Kerrie waited in the departure lounge. Someone touched her arm and she turned to find a tall, dark-haired glamazon at her elbow.

"That's the Morrigan!" I blurted.

Even in her guise as Miss Moore the Morrigan turned heads. It wasn't just her height, or the dark mane of hair that flowed down to her waist, shining as if she'd just stepped out of a shampoo commercial. There was something in the way she walked, a commanding yet sensual aura. If you could bottle that you'd make a fortune.

"You dropped something." Her smile had something predatory about it. Uh-oh. Kerrie should have been running like hell, not standing there being polite. The Morrigan held out a silver charm on a necklace.

"No, that's not mine …" Kerrie stared at the charm swinging on its chain until it seemed to fill her vision. It was a bird's feather, etched in detailed strokes despite its small size. Then she reached out. "Thank you."

I wanted to yell at her to stop as she fastened the thing around her neck, even though this had already happened and there was nothing we could do to change it.

"My pleasure," said the Morrigan, and if she had seemed beautiful before that was nothing to how she appeared now in Kerrie's dazzled vision. It was as if a curtain had been drawn back, revealing her true self, and she shone like diamonds.

Bleurgh. I couldn't think about diamonds the same way after last year. Probably more Sidhe trickery, just like those damn diamonds dripping from our mouths with every word, but Kerrie fell for it and fell hard. She seemed dazed, though it was hard to be sure, since we were seeing through her eyes. She stood rooted to the spot and watched the Morrigan until she was out of sight, and even then it was a long time before she moved.

"What the hell was that?" Bryan breathed into the silence.

Everyone stared at Kerrie. "I—I don't remember that."

"I'm sure you don't," said Mum, and her tone held its usual warmth. The smile she gave Kerrie was full of sympathy. "Are you still wearing that necklace she gave you?"

"Yes." Kerrie's hand stole to her chest and clutched at something concealed beneath her shirt.

"Take it off."

"But …" Mum's eyes bored into Kerrie's until she lifted her hands to the clasp at the back of her neck. There was a long pause, and her fingers started to tremble. "I—I can't."

"Kyle," said Mum, and the big man nodded and pushed Kerrie's hands out of the way.

In a minute the charm was swinging free, clutched in his fist, and Kerrie let out a startled cry.

"Oh, God!" She covered her mouth with her hands, and her eyes were huge with horror. "I remember."

Chapter Twelve

The car pulled up in College Street and the three of us got out. Sydney was putting on another scorching summer's day, and the temperature was already well above thirty degrees Celsius though it was only ten in the morning.

Saint Mary's Cathedral loomed over us, its many towers and spires piercing the blue sky above. It was built of the same warm sandstone as many of Sydney's grand old buildings and almost glowed in the sunshine. Massive doors, banded in iron, stood closed at the top of a grand flight of steps. I got goose bumps just looking at those steps. Last time I'd been here, this whole plaza below the steps had been carpeted with the Morrigan's damn black birds, all rustling and squawking in the world's creepiest chorus, while Zac, Sona, and I had stood up there, doing our best to save CJ from the Morrigan.

I sighed. Best not to think about Zac. Even the memory of the terrible danger we'd shared made me miss him. He'd still been at school for the first couple of days this week, very determinedly pretending he hadn't seen me every time I passed him, and the sight of his familiar face turned away from me had broken my heart all over again. It had been all I could do not to run after him and tell him I'd changed my mind. Only reminding myself that I was doing this to save him had enabled me to remain strong.

At least he was flying out this weekend, so I wouldn't have to see him again.

"It says it's closed for repair," CJ said, pointing at a sign that stood in front of the doors.

"Good," said Mum. "Less onlookers that way."

She led the way up the stairs, striding out confidently, as if she wasn't about to attempt to remove one of the four great treasures from its long hiding spot.

"Shouldn't you have a seeker with you for this?" I asked, glancing back at Kyle, who was already easing the big car out into the traffic again. He'd be back for us when we were ready, but I'd have felt more comfortable if he'd stayed. Kerrie's experience with the Morrigan had me jumpy as hell, half-expecting to find random Sidhe lurking around every corner.

"I don't need any assistance." Mum shot me a perceptive look. "You don't have to come if you'd rather not. I just thought it would be interesting for you to see. It's not something that happens very often, and one day you will have an important role to play among the warders. It would be good experience for you."

Her gaze included both of us in that "you", but CJ's face clouded over. We both knew she could never be a warder. Not unless they got over their ridiculous obsession with latency.

Mum tried the doors, but they didn't budge. I glanced around, but no one was taking any notice. If they did, they'd probably only assume we were tourists who couldn't read the sign.

"This way," said Mum.

She led us back down the steps and around to a much less imposing entrance on the side. This was also locked, but Mum removed something that looked like a tiny Hendrix counter from her handbag. Instead of a sensor it had a small metal device on the end, and she inserted it into the lock. A tiny pink spark flew from the lock, and the door opened with a click.

"What's that?" I asked as she tucked it back into her bag.

"Handy little all-purpose tool," she said. "Think of it as the magical equivalent of the Swiss army knife."

I frowned. "But where do you get the aether to power it? From the vault?"

"Of course. Where else?"

"But what happens when the aether you've stored there runs out? You've been using it for a couple of hundred years now. It's not going to last forever, is it?"

She opened the door and we followed her into a small side chapel. "We're not wasteful. We only use it when it's important."

"You just used it to pick a lock. That doesn't seem like something worth wasting a precious resource on. You could have used an ordinary lock pick."

"I wouldn't know a lock pick if I fell over one." Her tone was a little tart. "And this is most certainly an occasion worth 'wasting' a little aether for. May I remind you we are here to retrieve the great spear of Lugh?"

She'd spoken softly, but her voice echoed in the empty cathedral. Her footsteps were loud too as she tapped her way across the tiles to another chapel. We followed, trying to walk more quietly. Mum definitely needed to work on her sneaking abilities.

I recognised this chapel. It held a giant painting of Jesus on the cross, with the centurion poking him in the side with a spear, to see if he was dead or not. On the other side of the cross stood Mary, looking up at her son with tortured eyes.

"About that," I said.

Mum marched right up to the painting and climbed the three red-carpeted steps beneath it. She paused, looking back at me. "Yes?"

"What happens if you and Dorian succeed in using the treasures to strengthen the anchors, and all the leaks are sealed, and yay, the Sidhe and their aether are locked away forever—and then you discover that you can't fix Dad and Sona and Sergei with the amount of aether you've got left?"

Her forehead creased into a tiny frown. "Is this why you're worried about wasting aether? There's no reason to think that will happen."

A kind of mini-altar covered in flowers stood on the top step, and she pushed the vases to one side and plonked her magical Swiss army knife machine down in their place.

"But let me ask you this," she continued. "What happens if we don't strengthen the anchors, because we're afraid for Dad and Sona and Sergei, and then the Sidhe break through and take back our world?" Her green eyes pinned me to the spot. "You are thinking of the people you love, which is only natural at your age. The warders must think of the whole world. But don't ever imagine that I have forgotten your father. We *will* get him back, honey. Trust me."

I nodded, not entirely convinced, but still a little reassured, and she turned away. For one horrified moment I thought she was going to hop up onto the altar herself, but she managed to stretch up and attach the metal tip of the device to the painting by standing on tiptoe.

"This doesn't seem very respectful," I muttered to CJ.

"Why do you care? We're not Catholics." Her tone was petulant. Probably still smarting at Mum's remarks about our shining future with the warders. Her face had that get-me-out-of-here look.

We were speaking in whispers, but Mum still heard.

"We're very grateful to the Catholics, and indeed, all believers," she said, without turning around. She was making some adjustments on her little machine. "It is their belief that makes places like this anathema to the Sidhe. Their belief has helped protect the spear all these years. But we must use that belief to keep them, and everyone else, safe. No disrespect is intended—but a little disrespect, if it is taken as such, is a small price to pay for that safety."

She pressed a button on the side of the machine, and it buzzed into life. There was no chanting in old Irish this time; it seemed we were using magicology here and not magic itself. The buzzing got louder and grew to a whine. I shifted uncomfortably. Someone was going to hear this.

"What are you doing?" I asked. *And why does it have to be so loud?*

"Dispelling the aether," Mum said. "Collecting it, actually. So it's not *wasted*."

She winked at me over her shoulder.

"What aether? Is there a hiding place behind the painting?" Maybe the painting wasn't even there, only an image of a painting, and the truth was something completely different. My imagination supplied a giant safe in the cathedral wall, large enough to hold the spear, complete with arcane locking devices and magical inscriptions.

"Nope."

Abruptly the machine ceased its whining noise and Mum uncoupled it from the painting. Then she slashed its metal tip across the palm of her hand.

"Eww, gross!" CJ recoiled as blood welled in a bright red line across Mum's skin. "What did you do that for?"

"The hiding place is *in* the painting." She squeezed her hand shut, coating her fingers with the blood. It must have hurt, but she was grinning with excitement. "And my blood is the key that unlocks it."

"That's disgusting."

"Why your blood?" I asked.

"Because I am a descendant of the mage who placed it here."

"That's kind of risky, isn't it? What if that line had died out? Or you'd been turned into a bear instead of Dad? The spear might be trapped in the painting forever."

"No, any of the other warders could have done it. It just would have been a little trickier for them. Watch this."

She rested her bloody hand on the painting, just above where the centurion's fist closed around the shaft of the spear. Nice. Someone was *not* going to be happy about that big bloody paw print in the middle of their painting.

For a moment nothing happened, though Mum was leaning

all her weight against her hand, as if she was trying to push right through the canvas.

"Is your hand *glowing*?" CJ moved forward, fascinated.

In a moment there was no doubt, as the glow intensified. Mum's hand was suffused with soft pink light that stood out like a beacon in the dim cathedral. And then the glow faded as her fingers pushed right into the painting and closed on the spear.

"Oh. My. God," breathed CJ.

I could only stare, open-mouthed, as Mum slowly withdrew her hand. Released from the painting, the spear rapidly grew from picture-sized to its real full length. The glow from Mum's hand winked out like a candle being snuffed as she grounded the butt on the carpet. The spear point was above her head. Its sharp tip caught the light from the windows and gleamed. How on earth were we going to sneak something that big out of here?

"What are you doing?" a voice behind us demanded.

I whirled around, my heart jumping into my throat, and found a grey-haired man glaring at us through thick black-rimmed glasses. He wore a plain white shirt and dark trousers—he might have been a priest or a caretaker.

"The cathedral is closed," he said. "How did you get in here? And what are you doing with that spear?"

"What spear?" Mum asked.

I looked at her, incredulous. There were times when brazening it out could work, but being caught holding a two-metre spear was not one of them.

"I know the cathedral's closed," she continued. "The archbishop asked me to look at the paintings while the repairs were underway."

"With a *spear*? What were you doing to that painting? I saw a light."

Oops.

"This is an ultra-violet wand." She held the spear out to him and I blinked. Somehow, since I'd last looked at it, the spear had shrunk to an inoffensive rod no longer than Mum's forearm. "I've been using it to examine all the paintings for damage."

She pressed a button on the side of the "wand" and it lit up with purple ultra-violet light. It was nothing like the pink glow of aether but the man frowned. Now he didn't seem as certain of what he'd seen.

"You had a spear," he said, but his voice lacked conviction.

"It's awfully dark in here," Mum said cheerfully. "I'm surprised you can see anything in this gloom. I assure you I don't have any spears. Not much call for them in the art restoration world."

I glanced from the man's confused face to the spear and back again. The burnt toffee scent of aether was so strong I wondered if he could smell it too. Mum continued to smile at him in a friendly way.

"Who are these girls?" he asked, scowling.

I couldn't help feeling sorry for him, though my heart was still hammering from the scare he'd given me. He found himself in that horrible position of having seen something that made no sense, and now he didn't know whether to trust his senses or give in to the far more likely scenario offered by the smiling lady. He probably couldn't shake the suspicion that he was being duped.

"They're doing work experience with me," Mum said.

Wow, I'd never realised what a convincing liar she was. Now I knew where CJ had gotten it from.

"And you are—?"

"Catherine O'Malley from Kennedy Art Restorations," she said, offering her hand to shake.

I cringed as he took it, until I realised the blood was all gone. There was no sign now of the cut she'd sliced into her palm.

"I think I'll stay and watch you work," he said.

"No need." Mum picked up her machine from the top of the altar and rearranged the vases as they had been before. "We're all done here for now. Tell the archbishop he can expect my report within the fortnight. Let's go, girls."

He nodded uncertainly as we followed Mum to the door. When I looked back he was still standing there.

Outside Mum closed the door then leaned back against it and heaved a dramatic sigh. "That was close! I nearly jumped through the roof when he sneaked up on us."

"Me too," I said. "How did you change the spear like that?"

It was still in its innocent "wand" shape, just a thin nondescript tube. No one would look twice at it.

"Just dumb luck that it still had enough aether in it from the extraction. All I had to do was tell it another shape and it transformed. Wouldn't work now, though. Transformation takes a lot of juice."

"But you spoke English. I thought magic used Old Irish."

She laughed. "Do you think they had a word for 'ultra-violet wand' in Old Irish? Fortunately, the spear takes the required form directly from the wielder's mind."

CJ took the spear from her and examined it closely. "Do art restorers really use ultra-violet wands in their work?"

"No idea," she said cheerfully. "I don't even know if such

things exist. But it sounded convincing, didn't it? How else was I going to explain the light he saw?"

Full points to Mum for improvising under pressure. I was impressed. "Will you have to change it back for it to work as an anchor?"

"I don't know." She contemplated the thin wand in CJ's hands with a frown. "I'll have to talk to Dorian, see what he thinks. Hopefully not—it would take a good portion of the aether we have stored in the vault." She grinned at me, flushed with the successful extraction. "And it's very important not to waste aether."

I smiled back. "So I've heard."

Chapter Thirteen

"Vi, wake up. It's time to go."

I groaned. "What time is it?"

"Six-thirty. Come on, before everyone else is awake."

Six-thirty on a Saturday morning. Had CJ ever gotten up that early on the weekend in her life? We'd had a late night too. Frida and Simon had flown back in with the sword, and everyone had crowded into the vault to see the three great treasures of the Sidhe lying there absorbing aether, together for the first time in over two hundred years.

A lead weight of guilt settled in my stomach as I forced my eyelids open and took in the picture of my fully-dressed sister, jiggling impatiently from foot to foot beside my bed. "I thought we were going to wait until this afternoon, when the park was full of people?"

"Change of plan. Get up."

"I don't know, Ceej." Now that the moment was here, all my logical objections to the plan came rushing back. We had no idea what we were doing. What if we got stuck in fairyland, or made everything worse? "Maybe this isn't such a great idea."

She put her hands on her hips and glared down at me. "You can't back out now. Mum's already left for the airport. She'll be in Townsville by lunchtime with the sword. Everyone will be in position for the ritual to go ahead tonight. If we don't get that cauldron back today, it'll be too late for Dad and Sona. And Sergei," she added as an afterthought.

I sat up and put my feet on the floor. She was right. Much as I hated the idea, I couldn't see any other way to restore the fairytale victims to normal. All the warders had was a lot of wishful thinking. No ideas. I couldn't bear to lose Sona, trapped in a drugged sleep and plagued with dancing nightmares.

And a little voice in my head whispered it might already be too late for Dad. I hadn't been back to see him since the day he swiped at me. Not because I was scared, but because I couldn't stand to see him like that—just a big dumb animal, with no trace of my quick-witted father left. Mum said sometimes he was more like his old self, but even seeing him that way once had been too much for me.

"Have you had breakfast?" I asked as I dressed in jeans, a dark T-shirt, and hiking boots. CJ was wearing the same thing.

"No. I've packed protein bars."

We each had a backpack loaded with bottled water, bread, fruit, and cheese, plus two hunting knives CJ had pilfered from among Sergei's belongings. No one would miss them. I'd managed to talk her out of trying to steal guns. Apart from the fact that neither of us had ever used one, I thought the cold iron of the knives might be a better deterrent against fairies. She'd also packed some rope and a compass, though I doubted the compass would be much use in the fairy realm. Which way was north when you weren't in the real world?

She hovered impatiently as I tied my shoes.

"Ready?" she asked, the minute I stood up.

I took a deep breath. "Yes."

She could tell my heart wasn't in it, but she wasn't looking for enthusiasm, only agreement. She grabbed my hand and towed me out of the room as if afraid I'd change my mind if we didn't get going straight away.

Gretel came out of the kitchen as we passed, and her eyebrows rose in surprise at the backpacks we carried.

"Where are you two off to so early?"

"Thought we'd go hiking," CJ said breezily, not letting me stop. "The weather forecast says it's going to be a beautiful day."

"Have fun."

"We will!" CJ waved cheerily as she all but pushed me into the stairwell.

We made it out onto the street without seeing anyone else. CJ set a fast pace. With my shorter legs, I had to scurry to keep up with her.

"Slow down!" I begged as we hit the steps at the bottom of the climb up to the Observatory. "What's the rush?"

"It's nearly changeover time." For the last few days, she'd been tracking the movements of the seekers assigned to watching the park, and she'd discovered that the morning shift replaced the night shift some time between six forty-five and seven o'clock.

"Why are we doing this now instead of this afternoon? Now we'll have two seekers wondering what the hell we're doing instead of just one being distracted by fifty brides."

"If we time it right, they'll be too busy chatting and comparing notes on their iPads to notice what we're up to."

She sounded confident, but I noticed she still wasn't answering my question. Just as no one could fail to notice the two of us lurking around the fence of the Observatory at this time of day. Sure, we passed a few joggers, but we'd need a busload of schoolkids or a marching band to provide a big enough diversion, and I couldn't see that happening. A sense of foreboding filled me. CJ was hiding something.

By the time we got to the top of the stairs I was having serious second thoughts. It was only the thought of Dad and Sona that kept my feet moving across the damp grass towards the fence.

Simon stepped out of the shadow of the bandstand as we approached.

"What are you two doing here?"

"We're heading out for the day," said CJ. "Dorian said if we saw you to tell you to come in."

"What does he want, do you know?"

"No idea. Probably something to do with the ritual. You're helping him tonight, aren't you?"

"Yeah." He glanced at his watch. "Kyle should be here soon. I'll head off as soon as he comes."

"Oh, look!" CJ pointed over his shoulder. "Here he comes now. Why don't you walk down to meet him?"

I couldn't believe it was that easy. He turned and strode off to where Kyle was just appearing out of the tunnel under the bridge. No one ever expected CJ to lie; apparently her angelic face was too trustworthy.

I watched his retreating back. "Was that smart? What's he going to think when he reports in to Dorian and Dorian says he didn't ask to see him? You've just made us look suspicious."

"So? When we come back with the cauldron no one will give a crap. Now tell me where you can smell aether the strongest."

I headed for the fence closest to the statue of old Hans. Burnt toffee hung on the morning air, and my stomach rumbled hungrily. I shifted a few steps either side to be sure. Yep, this was the spot.

"Here."

"Great. You keep an eye on Simon and Kyle. Tell me if they're watching us."

The two men still had their heads together over Simon's iPad, and the bulk of the bandstand between us partially shielded what we were doing.

"Okay. And what are you going to do?"

She pulled out the mirror and blew gently on its reflective surface, her breath fogging the glass. A faint pink glow radiated from it, as if it was feeding on the aether here. I glanced back toward Simon and Kyle, sudden panic fluttering in my chest. We must be crazy to even contemplate this.

"Quick, give me your hand."

She shoved the mirror at me and I closed my fingers around the handle. She hung onto it too, her fingers pressed against mine.

Streamers of pink light twisted off it like mist, but when I looked into the glass I gasped. There was a face in the mirror, but it wasn't mine. A man stared back at me. He lifted a lazy hand and waved in a mocking gesture.

He was a golden figure. His skin was tanned golden brown, his hair was a rich tawny brown, and his eyes were the same colour. He even wore a jacket of the same honey-gold shade.

"Is that Ariel?"

"Yes." She angled the mirror back toward herself and smiled at him.

"Funny. He doesn't look like the little mermaid."

She shot me a withering look. "Ha ha. Ariel was around long before Disney started rewriting fairy tales."

Well, at least Disney gave them happy endings. I bet if they ever did the Red Shoes there'd be no screaming and dancing to death involved.

The pink light streamed from the mirror, making me sick with dread. It was forming itself into a jagged line that hung in the air in front of us. Now that the moment was here I was fast losing confidence in the plan, such as it was. Ariel had the same arrogant, otherworldly look that Puck had had, and look where trusting him had got me. We were mad to put ourselves in this creature's power.

Someone shouted behind us. CJ twisted around, pink lights reflecting in her eyes, and over her shoulder I saw Simon and Kyle sprinting across the grass toward us. Thank God. We wouldn't have to go through with this.

"Let's *go*." CJ pushed me hard, and I went sprawling to the ground beneath her. There was a pink flash, and the sky reeled. For a moment I thought I would throw up, and then the feeling passed.

I pushed CJ off me and sat up, feeling unaccountably shaky. Then I looked around.

"Oh, shit. What have we done?"

CJ scrambled to her feet, spread her arms and laughed up at the rosy pink sky. "Welcome to fairyland."

"Oh, my God." I stood too. We were in the middle of a lush meadow, full of flowers. Perhaps "clearing" might have been a better word, for there were trees all around us. Not the kind of trees I was used to, though. No gum trees here—they were massive oaks, their green so vibrant it almost hurt the eye. Something moved in the shadows under the trees, and my heart started hammering, but it was only a white doe. She stared at us, then appeared to decide we were no threat, and dropped her head to crop at the grass beneath the tree again.

"Isn't it beautiful?" CJ said, her eyes bright as she took it all in.

The mirror lay winking in the sunlight on the grass, and I swooped on it. But no golden Sidhe looked back at me any more, only my own rather wild-eyed reflection. No pink light streamed off it either. It was just a mirror, and there was no sign now of the rip it had created in the fabric of reality.

"How the hell do we get out of here?" I asked.

CJ shrugged. "We can worry about that later. First we have to get what we came for."

"Do you have any idea where the cauldron is?"

It would be too much to hope that Ariel might have given away such sensitive information.

"Nope. But Ariel knows we're here. He'll come find us soon, and then we can start looking."

"What if he doesn't want to help us? What are we going to do?"

"Relax, would you?"

She took off her backpack and began pulling things out of it. Protein bars, apples, a length of rope, the compass. The needle of the compass whirled wildly, desperately seeking a north that no longer existed.

And then she dived into the pack again and when she brought her hand out it held a horribly familiar shape.

"Oh, my God. You *didn't*." I buried my face in my hands, hardly knowing whether to laugh or cry. "You brought the spear of Lugh *here*? When the Sidhe already have the cauldron?" I thought I could see now what Ariel wanted from my sister. "Are you completely *insane*?"

CJ threw the spear, still in its ultraviolet wand disguise, at my feet. "I thought you'd be pleased."

"Pleased? This whole problem started because the Sidhe got hold of one of the four treasures. And you think it's a good idea to home-deliver another one? Why didn't you just save us all a lot of time and bring the sword and the stone too?"

I bent down and picked it up, and felt the thing shiver under my hand like something alive. The sensation was so creepy I almost dropped it again.

CJ folded her arms crossly. "If you could just stop yelling at me for five seconds and think about it—the spear can take any form you like. They don't even have to know we've got it. It could be very handy."

"For what?"

"I don't know." Her voice was sullen. "We'll just have to see what comes up, won't we? Why don't you try turning it into something else, if you're so worried?"

I looked at the spear doubtfully. Now I could see the reason for CJ's haste this morning, and why she hadn't wanted to tell me the reason for the change in plan. I couldn't believe she'd managed to sneak one of the four great treasures out of the vault without getting caught.

The vault! I frowned at her. "How much aether did it use?"

"How should I know? I can't smell the stupid stuff like some people." Maybe not, but the vault had common old garden-variety read-outs on it too, including something that looked like an enormous petrol gauge in a car, with markings from "full" to "empty".

"I wonder if you left them enough to manage their ritual?" At least that would be something, if her theft had managed to halt the anchoring ceremony. Not that it would be exactly helpful if the spear ended up in the hands of the Sidhe. I rubbed tiredly at my temples, where a headache was threatening. As if today hadn't been challenging enough already.

She shrugged. "They'll probably have to wait for us to get back anyway. I doubt they can do the ritual with only two of the treasures. They'll forgive us when we bring back the cauldron too."

If only I shared her confidence.

I reached for the spear again, bracing myself this time against the strange shiver at its touch. "How exactly am I supposed to change this?"

"Mum said you just think of the form you want it to take. It should be easy enough for *you*." Her voice held a hint of bitterness, which I ignored. I was in no mood to feel sorry for her lack of latency now.

What would be a good form to hide the spear? Maybe I

should just leave it as it was. It wasn't as if the Sidhe would recognise it.

It *was* kind of heavy though. I glared at the wand for a moment, and then it bucked in my hand and I dropped it with a squeak.

"Cool!" CJ swooped on the phone that now lay in the grass. "Does it work?"

I hardly heard her. A strange sensation overwhelmed me, a tickling that swept through my whole body. As if my blood had been replaced by soft drink, and was fizzing through my veins. I could feel the bubbles bursting.

I sat down abruptly. CJ eyed me worriedly.

"Are you all right?"

"Not … sure." My voice sounded funny too, echoing hollowly in my ears. The smell of burnt toffee hit me, so hard it made my eyes water, and when I looked up everything was outlined in a soft pink glow.

I don't know how long I sat there admiring the glowing grass. Every blade stood out clearly, every flower's beauty was magnified by the light surrounding it. I hardly dared look at the trees. Their shimmering leaves were overwhelming. Fairyland had looked pretty before, but that was nothing to how it appeared now.

At last I realised CJ was yelling in my ear and shaking me. She'd bruised my shoulders before I came back to myself. I looked at her in surprise.

"You're not glowing."

"I'm not what? What's wrong with you?"

I looked at my own arm, outlined in a soft rose glow. There

was nothing wrong with me. She was the one with the problem. Why was she the only dull thing in the middle of such beauty?

"Stop that!" She shook me again. Her voice held a note of panic. "Will you snap out of it?"

"Sorry." I shut my eyes to block out the glowing world. It must be the aether that I could see—but why hadn't I seen it before? It wasn't until I'd changed the spear that it became visible.

I opened my eyes and looked for the spear. The phone lay on the grass. CJ must have dropped it in her panic. The light it gave off was so blinding I couldn't look directly at it.

"Houston, we have a problem."

"You mean apart from you going all zombie on me and freaking me out? What now?"

"We can't hide the spear from the Sidhe. It's, um … giving off magic vibes."

"Magic vibes? That's a thing now?"

"Yep." I ignored the scepticism in her tone. "Definitely a thing. It's like I can see a whole other spectrum, and the spear is just shouting *look at me* on that spectrum."

"How come you didn't mention this magical spectrum before?"

"It kind of only just appeared when I changed the spear."

"Huh. Well, it doesn't even work as a phone. No signal." She picked it up rather gingerly and held it out to show me. "Are you sure the Sidhe can see this magical spectrum too?"

I nodded. "Pretty sure."

"So how are we going to disguise it?" She slipped it back into her backpack. "Does that help?"

"No." The backpack shone like a beacon. I was surprised the doe on the edge of the clearing wasn't looking for her sunglasses already. CJ took the phone back out and turned it over in her hand. I could hardly believe she could stare straight at it like that, though I'd been able to myself just a few moments ago. Now it made my eyes water.

I held out my hand. "Give it to me."

It was like a mini-sun shifted from her hand to mine. Even when I closed my eyes I could still sense it, blazing away. I felt the tingling again, whizzing through my veins. Was that aether? I cracked one eyelid and squinted at the phone. Was I glowing brighter than before?

It was hard to tell with the phone a white fire in my hand, but it gave me an idea.

"Take my hand," I said, "and put your other hand on the spear. I'm going to change it again."

"To what?" she asked, but she did as I said.

When we were joined I changed the spear to a battery, and imagined us as a circuit for the aether to rush through, from the spear to me, through CJ and back to the spear again. Hey, it was worth a try.

CJ shifted uncomfortably. "What the hell is that?"

"What?"

"It feels like ants are running around under my skin."

"That's good! No, don't take your hand away."

"I can't stand it."

"Just a little longer," I urged. The spear was noticeably dimmer, and CJ had begun to shine just like everything else. "Do you see anything different?"

She looked around. "Like what?"

That was a little disappointing. It didn't change her lack of latency then. She was brimming with the raw stuff of magic, but she still couldn't see it. I'd hoped that filling her with aether might help. But at least siphoning some off had toned down the brilliance of the spear. I could look at it now without wincing.

"Okay, that's it." Abruptly CJ let go of my hand. "So, are we good now? Is the spear still shouting on the magical spectrum thingy?"

"Not as much. Maybe I can get rid of some more." My circuit idea might conduct aether to other objects besides people. I sat down among the flowers. They were nothing like any flowers I'd ever seen, more like a fantasy artist's depiction of flowers, alien but beautiful. I picked one, a vivid orange with a burst of glowing emerald at its centre. The green was almost exactly the colour of the dress I'd worn to the formal last year.

That was the night Zac had first kissed me. I sighed, remembering the warmth in his voice as he'd said that he thought green might be his new favourite colour, the look in his brown eyes as he'd bent over me. His eyes were the colour of chocolate, a deep rich brown that I never tired of gazing into. I clenched my fist on the delicate flower stem as my own eyes filled with unexpected tears. There was no point pining for Zac, though he would have loved to have seen this. I'd done the right thing, and he was safe now because of it, tucked away in London somewhere far from the Morrigan's reach.

"What did you do to that poor flower?" CJ asked. "It was much prettier before."

I looked down. The flower clenched in my fist was green and orange no longer. Instead it was brown, the exact shade of Zac's eyes.

And I hadn't been touching the spear.

Chapter Fourteen

A flash of white under the trees caught my eye: the white doe, bounding away into the forest. I scrambled to my feet, shoving the spear, in its current battery incarnation, into my back pocket as I did. The brown flower I let fall to the ground, where it glowed brighter than its prettier companions.

My heart was thumping. I'd worked magic. I remembered the feel of it, the sensation of something shifting inside, from that time in Puck's cell when the Morrigan's origami bird came to life in my hand. *Throw your heart at it*, he'd said. *You have to want it to change.* But that had been trickery. This was real; something I'd done all by myself. It was as if the spear had unlocked something inside me, and now the aether was free to fizz through my bloodstream. I'd never felt so alive.

CJ had noticed the doe fleeing too.

"Is someone coming?" She shouldered her pack and turned a circle in the vivid grass, checking the perimeter of the clearing.

"Could be your boyfriend." I should have been afraid, but I felt like shouting it to the sky: *I could do magic*. I hardly cared how many Sidhe discovered us now. I felt invincible, drunk on aether.

Ariel stepped out of the trees, and the sunshine fell on his golden head like a spotlight. He was even more beautiful in real life than he'd appeared in the mirror.

He opened his arms.

"CJ," he said, and his voice was as gorgeous as the rest of him, deep and husky.

CJ dropped me like a hot potato and fled across the meadow to throw herself into his arms.

"Ariel!"

He laughed as she cannoned into him, then cupped her face in his hands and covered it with kisses. "I'm glad to see you, too."

I cleared my throat noisily. I'd never seen her greet anyone like that in my life. She was acting more like a hysterical puppy than anyone with a shred of self-esteem had any right to. If this was an act, she might want to tone it down.

"Ariel, this is my sister, Violet."

He let go of her long enough to sweep a deep flourish of a bow. "A beautiful name for a beautiful girl."

He needn't think he was going to charm me. I'd been Zac-proofed. Zac might not be as good-looking as this guy, but he was worth a hundred of him.

"It's a thrill to be able to welcome you to my world," he continued. "Let me take you to my home. You can rest and replenish yourselves there."

"Actually we're not the least bit tired," she said, smiling up at him through her lashes. "Couldn't you show us around a bit? I'd love to meet your king and queen. I've heard their palace is beautiful."

We'd figured that the cauldron was most likely to be in the palace. It was somewhere to start looking, at least. Maybe it would blaze on the magical spectrum the way the spear had done. That would help.

He frowned. "Their majesties are very busy people. I don't know if an audience could be arranged."

CJ pouted at him. "Oh, please! Couldn't you at least try? I'm so longing to see it."

Now it was his turn to pout. "I thought it was me you were longing to see."

She traced her fingers across his chest playfully. "Of course! But it's not every day a girl gets to go to fairyland. I want to see as much as I can."

"Then come to my house first. While you rest there I will see what I can arrange."

She clapped her hands. "Wonderful!"

His insistence on us going to his house bothered me. Why was he so anxious to get us there? Probably not for any reason we would like—but there was nothing we could do about it. We were basically at his mercy. Our best weapons here were CJ's smile and her fluttering eyelashes, and she was wielding them to good effect so far. At least he didn't seem suspicious.

"We can't stay long, though," I said. I'd heard enough about fairy bargains to be wary. I didn't want to be trapped at his house for weeks while he pretended to arrange an audience for us. "No more than a couple of hours."

"Of course." He gave me a half-bow, though I couldn't help feeling the jerk was laughing at me. "I have no wish to deny you the pleasures of Tir na nÓg."

Then he offered his arm to CJ. She laid her fingers on it like a grand lady and he led us across the meadow towards the trees. I trudged along behind, thinking dark thoughts about the Sidhe and their smarmy ways.

"Speaking of time," I said as we passed under the shadow of the mighty oaks, "how much time is passing in our world while we're here?"

He laughed. "You've heard the stories, then. But you have nothing to fear. Since your mages anchored Tir na nÓg and trapped us here, our time stream has been likewise anchored to yours. Time will continue for you here exactly as it does in your world."

"So we won't go back and find ten years has passed?"

He laid a hand on his heart. "I swear it by the Bright Lady."

He tugged CJ's hand and we continued deeper into the woods. There was no path, but he seemed to know exactly where he was going, and tree branches leaned out of his way as we passed. I glanced back, wondering how we would ever find our way back to the clearing without him, but it was already out of sight. All I could do was follow and hope that he meant us no harm. At least not immediately.

Not that I had any reason to trust him. He could be lying through his teeth about the time stream thing, and we'd get home only to find that everyone we knew was dead and the world had moved on without us. Still, for every story like that there were plenty more where stupid young men had danced the night away in a fairy mound and returned no worse for wear. I just had to hope we'd be among the lucky ones.

We were certainly going to need plenty of luck to pull this

off. Ariel was hardly likely to help us get home with the stolen cauldron, unless we could somehow manage to disguise the fact that we'd taken it. Far more likely that we'd be needing to leave in an awful hurry, with a lot of pissed off Sidhe on our tails. Would we really be able to wish our way home using the power of the cauldron?

It had worked just fine when I had wished for condensors to fight the Morrigan with. And there'd certainly be no lack of aether here. I could still feel it fizzing in my blood, and see it glowing in every perfect leaf and flower we passed. But for the first time it occurred to me that all the wishes I'd heard of had been for concrete objects: something that could be physically pulled from the cauldron. We could hardly pull the whole human world from its depths and step right in.

Could we use the mirror without Ariel? Magic had a lot to do with the power of the user's wishing. I guess that was why so many fairy tales focused on three wishes. You had to throw your heart at it, as Puck had said. Gretel said it worked on emotion, the stronger the better, which was a kind of wishing, I guess. And also on blood.

The blood in my veins seemed to have the special sauce ingredient, whatever it was. Enough to have changed the spear's form—and that flower. Would I be able to wish our way home?

"How much further?" I asked after some time.

"Why? Are you in a hurry?" Ariel threw an amused glance over his shoulder, and I felt suddenly afraid he knew exactly why we were here. Did he know about the spear riding in my back pocket too? "Is there somewhere else you'd rather be? Surely you're not bored of the Sunlit Land already!"

"Of course not. It's beautiful. But I'm tired and we've been walking for a while."

"Not much further," he promised. "Then you can rest."

It really was beautiful, more like a Hollywood impression of a wood than a real one. There were no weeds and brambles fighting for space under the trees, ready to snag the clothes of passing travellers. Moss and flowers shared the space between the great trees' roots, and their spreading branches provided dappled shade. Over everything the glow of aether lay like glitter. There were even little toadstools, their caps bright red and spotted with white, growing in clusters here and there. Classic fairytale stuff.

I had to admit, there was something thrilling about being here, despite the danger. How many people got the chance to see something like this? I felt like I was walking through a children's book illustration. The grass was so impossibly green, and looked so soft, I wanted to take off my shoes and wiggle my toes in it. I noticed Ariel went barefoot.

Off to the right I caught a glimpse of blue among all the greens and browns.

"What's that?"

"What?" Ariel turned to see where I was pointing. "Oh, nothing. Come, we're almost home."

I looked closer, ignoring his *hurry up* gesture. "No, there's somebody there." A figure was bent over between two roots of an oak. Looking at something on the ground, or spying on us? "Who is it?"

"Just a traveller, lost in the woods."

"Shouldn't we help him, then?" I started toward the person in blue. They still hadn't moved, and something about their stillness made me uneasy.

"Truly, there's no need to concern yourself." He caught at my arm but I pulled free, determined to see for myself.

I stopped when I was close enough to see the figure clearly. It was a man, dressed simply but in an old-fashioned style, in a blue shirt and brown pants. He wore a cap but no shoes, and he was bending over, reaching for one of the cute little toadstools.

And he hadn't shifted from that position the whole time I'd been watching him.

"Hello?" I said.

Ariel joined me, CJ at his side. "He can't hear you."

"Why not? What's wrong with him?"

"He is one of the Lost Ones. He stumbled into Tir na nÓg, or perhaps was led here in mischief, a long time ago."

"Why isn't he moving?"

Ariel sighed. "He is, but he is caught in a slower time stream. He has probably been a month reaching for that toadstool, and it might be another month more before he actually touches it."

CJ's eyes widened. "That's horrible!"

"How so? From his perspective, time moves normally. He doesn't suffer."

"But … his family. His life. What happens when he goes home and finds it's all gone?"

"How should he go home? Your warders have made it impossible for anyone to leave this place." A blackness flitted briefly over his features. It was the first time I'd seen a crack in his mask.

"I thought you said the time streams were the same between our worlds?" We'd barely been here an hour and already I'd caught him in a lie.

"And so they are," he said, all golden smiles again. So

smarmy. "The time streams have been aligned since your warders anchored our realm to theirs. Before that, it was a different story. Then, a man might wander into the fairy realm and sleep away a hundred human years in a single night."

So this guy had been here since before the warders created the Sidhe prison? I stared in horror at the bending man. "You mean he's been stuck like that for two centuries?"

CJ moved forward, arm outstretched. "Can't we wake him?"

Ariel jerked her back. "Don't touch him, or you might be drawn into the same time stream." She recoiled sharply. "He is beyond our aid, unfortunately."

"But there must be something you can do. Can't your king and queen change the time streams or something?"

"I see this has upset you." He stroked her face tenderly and leaned in for a kiss. "Let's be on our way."

I scowled at the back of his golden head as he drew her gently away. Pity I couldn't find a nice slow time stream to push *him* into. Lying bastard. The damn Sidhe were popping out of fairyland faster than you could play Whack-a-Mole. Why shouldn't this guy be able to leave?

I turned all my anger at Ariel on the poor toadstool guy. He should be able to reach that stupid fungus. He *should* be able to find his way back to the human world. I wished it so hard that I saw bright aether streaming from my outstretched fingers to form a glowing nimbus around the bending figure.

"Come on, Vi," CJ called. They were some distance ahead already.

As I turned to follow them the man's hand closed on the toadstool.

Chapter Fifteen

We stepped out of the forest into a small clearing, small enough that only the very centre of it received direct sunlight. In that patch of sun, as if in a spotlight, a pavilion made of a silken sky-blue fabric was set up. The sides were rolled up to show a floor heaped with bright cushions around a low central table.

CJ drew in a stunned breath. "This is where you *live?*"

I was a bit surprised too. I mean, it was pretty, but kind of lacking on the amenities side. Where was the kitchen? Or the bathroom? Or even some proper furniture? Lounging around on cushions sounded very decadent and all, but I, for one, would soon start to long for an actual chair—not to mention a bed.

I couldn't believe CJ sounded so impressed. She was the queen of the makeup mirror, after all. And where did he keep all his clothes? Wardrobe options were a must in a well-designed home.

"No." He smiled fondly down at her. "This is just a summer retreat."

"It's amazing. You must be a prince!"

I had to check to see if she was pulling his leg, but her expression was completely serious. She was a better actress than I'd thought.

He laughed. "No, not a prince. Not even close. Merely a humble messenger, at your service."

He swept her a deep bow. Humble messenger, my ass. There was nothing humble about this guy. He was so impressed with himself I didn't know what he even needed CJ for.

No, that wasn't true. I knew exactly what he needed her for, and it wasn't anything to do with a deep-seated desire to have a pretty girl follow him around oohing and aahing. He was using her against the warders. Maybe he'd influenced her to bring him the spear, or maybe that was her own horrible idea, but if it wasn't the spear he was after, he had some other plan. And it wasn't going to be anything we humans would like.

"Come, sit down and rest." He led us to the pavilion and settled CJ on a pile of cushions at his side.

Then he clapped his hands, and the weirdest looking creature I'd ever seen appeared. It looked like a hedgehog on two legs, if hedgehogs were the size of a six-year-old child, and it wore a dress of faded green with a ragged hem. Its little pointed face was cute, in an ugly sort of way, framed by soft quills curving up from its head, and it scampered up to Ariel and bobbed that head in a nervous approximation of a bow.

"What is *that?*" CJ recoiled a little from the hedgehog girl, though she seemed harmless and even more nervous of us than my sister was of her. The little black nose sniffed the air in CJ's direction doubtfully.

"This is Dewdrop." Dewdrop looked up at the sound of her name and bobbed her head even more vigorously than before, casting wary sidelong glances up at Ariel's face. "She is my servant."

"But what is she? Is she a Sidhe too?" CJ's expression suggested she'd have trouble believing Dewdrop and Ariel belonged to the same race.

"She is a Fomorian. Something like a cousin of ours, if you will."

My sister didn't look convinced.

"Bring food for our guests," Ariel said, and Dewdrop did some more anxious bobbing, then scurried away.

"Thanks for the offer, but we brought our own." I opened my backpack and pulled out two apples, passing one to CJ.

"That's right." She crunched into the apple and my stomach rumbled. I'd forgotten about breakfast, but it hadn't. "No need to worry about us."

"It's no trouble," he said.

Maybe not for him. He was lying around on a big fat pile of cushions, while poor little Dewdrop toiled back toward us balancing an enormous tray in her delicate furred hands, heaped high with fruits and little cakes and—oh, God!—freshly baked bread. The smell was divine, and my stomach rumbled again, loud enough for Ariel to hear.

He smirked at me. "Sure I can't tempt you to try something? A slice of bread slathered with freshly churned butter, perhaps, or one of these delightful little cakes?"

I bit into my apple, flooding my mouth with sweet juice. He could take his little cakes and shove them where the sun didn't shine.

"No, thank you."

Dewdrop set the tray on the low table, but she lost control of its weight at the last moment and it thumped down gracelessly. One perfect fuzzy globe of an apricot rolled off the table onto the cushions, and Ariel straightened, a nasty glitter in his eyes. Dewdrop cringed away from him, eyes downcast, but if she was expecting a blow it never came. He merely picked up the apricot and bit into it with his perfect white teeth.

"You may go," he said, and the hedgehog girl hurried away as if she couldn't believe her luck.

Maybe when there were no witnesses to impress he was less lenient with clumsy servants. I watched him lick apricot juice from his fingers and laugh with CJ, and had a hard time remembering last time I'd met anyone I liked less. Even Josh Johnson, CJ's last boyfriend, had only been a jerk, not a violent jerk. The little hedgehog girl had seemed so frightened.

I took a swig from my water bottle and eyed the food heaped on the table. It looked ordinary enough. In fact, some of his precious little cakes were oddly lopsided, as if Dewdrop might have made them herself, and the icing had started oozing down the side in a rather unappetising way, as if they were melting.

"Please, join me. Eat your fill."

"We've heard what happens to people who eat while they're here," I said.

"Ah." A sheepish grin flitted over his face, like a little boy caught with his hand in the cookie jar. "Well, you can't believe everything you hear, you know."

Right. Like *that* was convincing.

He seemed to realise he was losing me, because he arranged

his face into more serious lines. "Truly, Violet, even if I wanted to do you harm—and I assure you I do not!—you are perfectly safe from me now. The laws of hospitality protect you."

"Really? What laws are those?"

"You are my guest, protected by guest-rite. Even if you were to leap up and slit poor Dewdrop's throat in front of me"—he smiled, as if the idea held a certain appeal—"as your host I could not lift a finger against you. We have shared a meal, and that means your safety is my honour."

CJ smiled dreamily up at him. She was stretched out on the cushions, her head in his lap. "I feel perfectly safe with you."

"And glad I am to hear it." He bent over to drop a kiss on her lips.

Somehow I wasn't reassured. I knew how the Sidhe loved to split hairs and shape seemingly innocent words to mean something completely different. *We have shared a meal,* he said. Had we? Did eating two different things, merely while sitting together, constitute sharing a meal? And I noticed his talk of safety didn't include "safe return home". So he wasn't going to stick a knife into us? Great, but promises like that weren't worth much if he meant to keep us here forever.

"What about the other Sidhe?" I asked.

"What other Sidhe?"

"All of them. We haven't shared a meal with them, have we? What's to stop one of them trying to harm us?"

"Your sister is so suspicious," he complained. CJ stroked his cheek in apology. "You are determined to think the worst of us, aren't you? It makes me wonder why you ever ventured into our lands if you think so poorly of us."

He eyed me expectantly.

To steal the cauldron back from you probably wouldn't be an appropriate answer at this point.

"We're trying to find a cure for our father." It was the truth, after all. "Your people cursed him. We want to persuade them to lift the curse, as the Morrigan lifted ours."

He arched one golden eyebrow. "Did she? Well, she must have had her reasons. The Morrigan isn't one for handing out favours to all and sundry. But you may find it difficult to persuade one of the High Sidhe to lift a curse, unless you have something to offer them."

When he smiled like that I felt sure he knew all about the spear, but other times I decided he mustn't know, or he would have taken it already.

CJ pouted prettily at him. "Can't *you* lift the curse?"

"No, not I. I don't have that kind of power. One of the High Sidhe must have created the curse; only they can remove it."

"Then can you take us to them?"

"Of course." He smiled down at her. "And your untrusting sister will be pleased to know that once I have taken you to meet the king and queen and they have officially received you, the obligations of hospitality will extend to all Sidhe. You will be perfectly safe, and able to ask for any help you need. Of course, I can't guarantee they will give it to you. Still, two pretty girls like you—it will be hard to refuse you anything."

I snorted. I doubted the Morrigan, at least, would have any trouble.

He gently shifted CJ off his lap and rose to his feet in a graceful unfolding of legs. "Why don't you lovely ladies rest here.

I will go and beg an audience for you with their majesties."

CJ clung to his hand. "Don't be long."

He bent and kissed the back of her wrist. "I'll hurry straight back. You'll hardly notice I'm gone."

He waved as he headed into the trees, and CJ sank back in the pillows with a sigh. "Well, he took that better than I expected. I thought he'd throw a fit when you called him on eating his food."

"Yeah, me too. I thought that was the whole reason he was so insistent on us coming here."

"Maybe he just wanted to show off this place. Can you believe it? So much gold!"

I looked up, frowning. All I could see was the blue of the silken fabric gently swaying above us. "What gold?"

"On the pillars. And the plate." She gestured at the platter of food. "He must be incredibly rich."

"Um ... what pillars?" The pavilion appeared to be suspended from the trees above by thin ropes. There were certainly no pillars. And the plate was carved from a solid piece of timber. No wonder little Dewdrop had struggled with its weight.

She frowned at me. "What do you mean, *what pillars?*"

Either I was going crazy, or she was seeing something very different. I was about to ask her to describe what she could see, when Dewdrop crept back into view. She seemed more cheerful now, less furtive, and even smiled at me as she came right up to the table. A smiling hedgehog. That wasn't weird at all.

She was still shy, though. I took a piece of bread from the plate and held it out to her. "Would you like some food?"

"Oh, God, put that down." CJ groaned. "The smell is making my mouth water."

"Really?" I sniffed the bread curiously. It had smelled divine when Dewdrop first brought the platter out, but it had lost its scent now. In fact, it felt hard to the touch, as if it were stale, and not the fresh-baked delight I'd first imagined.

Dewdrop shook her head, the smile gone. Fair enough. Maybe she didn't want to eat something I'd been sniffing.

"How about some fruit? You must be hungry." She looked half-starved, poor little creature. Her arms were like matchsticks. But when I picked up an apricot she gave another decisive shake of her head.

"Nononononononono," she chittered in a squeaky little voice. She snatched the apricot from me and sliced it neatly open with her sharp little claws. "Bad food bad food."

She held it out in the palm of her furry hand.

CJ sat up, a look of revulsion on her face. "Ewww! What is that?"

A fat worm coiled its way around the stone of the apricot, through flesh gone dark and mushy.

"Bad food!" Dewdrop repeated in firm tones.

"That's disgusting," said CJ.

Worse than disgusting. The apricot Ariel had eaten hadn't looked like that. But now I looked closer, most of the fruit looked past its prime. He must have enchanted it before, to make it more appetising. And now the enchantment was wearing off.

But that didn't explain why CJ saw a different pavilion to the one I saw. I glanced around and noticed that some of the cushions were worn and stained, and there were rents in the faded blue fabric above us. God knew what CJ saw, with her talk of pillars of gold, but it was a far cry from the reality. Had he laid some enchantment on CJ, to impress her? Or did my own magic protect me from his?

Dewdrop let the rotten apricot fall to the grass, where she ground it into the dirt.

"Thank you." I opened my backpack and showed her the cheese and bread still inside. "Would you like some of our food?"

She nodded, and reached a shy hand toward the cheese. She broke it in half and offered me some. Together we munched, and a blissful look came over her whiskered face. When she finished she bobbed her funny little bow and hoisted the heavy plate of fairy food into her arms again. Before I could even say goodbye, she'd disappeared into the woods with it.

Just in the nick of time, too. Perhaps she had some sixth sense that warned her, because no sooner had she gone than Ariel turned up, smiling his insincere smile at my sister.

"I hope you are rested." If he noticed the magicked food was gone, he made no comment. "We are in luck. Their majesties will see you now."

Chapter Sixteen

The feast had already been going for some time, by the looks of things. We could hear laughter and happy shrieks long before we caught sight of the meadow where the Sidhe were gathered. One thing you could say for them: they sure knew how to party.

A pretty girl rushed past as we emerged from the trees, chased by some kind of goblin thing with big pointy ears like a bat, and covered in matted fur. Too busy laughing, neither of them paid us the slightest attention. The bat-eared guy would have knocked Ariel over if he hadn't sidestepped neatly out of his path. The girl slowed down to let her pursuer catch up, then rolled on the ground squealing as he tried to kiss her.

"Reminds me of some other parties we've been to," I said to CJ. At least I'd had Zac at those. I'd danced in his arms, my head nestled against his chest, his heart beating a steady rhythm in my ear. Where was he now? He could be halfway to England.

Someone was playing the fiddle, and someone else beat out the rhythm of a lilting tune that had a great crowd of Sidhe up and dancing. It wasn't my kind of party music—nothing beat "YMCA"—but they seemed to be enjoying it. It was obviously thirsty work, though, for many of the dancers had flopped to the ground around the edges of the dance, and were busy knocking back something that looked suspiciously like beer to take the edge off their thirst.

Well, that would make it easier to refuse to drink, at least. I'd been expecting something a little more exotic—ambrosia, or nectar, or even some kind of fairy wine. But beer? It didn't seem to fit. Though I guess it explained how so many young men had been lured into joining the fairy revels. What guy could resist a night of pretty girls and free beer?

Ariel led us past the dancers to a quieter area where a long table, large enough to have seated at least half the dancers, was spread with food of all kinds: great piles of fruit, cakes, meat of every sort—even a whole roast pig. It all looked and smelled delicious, so either this had a heavy-duty enchantment on it, or it was the real deal. My stomach grumbled a reminder that an apple and a piece of cheese wasn't enough to keep a girl going long.

At the head of the long table, and set back from it a little, two high-backed chairs stood side by side.

"Wow," CJ breathed.

The chairs were carved with flowers and leaves, and each had a green velvet cushion. They were made of a pretty honey-coloured wood, but "wow" seemed a bit generous.

"Lots of gold?" I asked.

"And so many jewels! They must be worth a fortune."

Ariel smiled at the look on her face. "The king and queen are not here yet, so we have time to dance, if you wish."

She shrugged off her backpack. "Sure. Let's go!"

He led her away to join the dancers and I grabbed her pack and set it on the bench beside me, feeling a little out of place among the party crowd. No one approached, which suited me just fine. There was only one guy I wanted to party with, and he wasn't here; I was more than happy to leave the partying to CJ.

The longer we stayed here, the less confident I felt of our chances of success. The task we'd set ourselves seemed almost impossible. We still had to find the cauldron, and then we had to get it out of here without anyone noticing. All while surrounded by powerful magic users who were on their home turf.

My gaze roved the length of the table, then stopped with a shock of recognition. Well, I could tick the first item off the list. At the head of the table, surrounded by bunches of grapes and delicate little pastries, sat a familiar black pot.

What the hell? One of the fabled four great treasures of their people, and they left it lying around where anyone could take it? I cast a furtive glance around. No one seemed to be watching it, or paying much attention to anything at all, apart from what a good time they were having.

Maybe I was wrong. Maybe it was just some old pot. But if it wasn't! My heart pounded. It would be so easy to wander over and shove it in my backpack. All I had to do then was figure out how the hell to get home again. Oh, and how to pry my sister out of Ariel's slimy clutches.

I looked out across the crowd of dancers. It took some time to pick her out of the sea of bobbing heads and whirling bodies, though her jeans and T-shirt did stand out among the riot of bright colours and pretty dresses that surrounded her. Her dark head snuggled in close to Ariel's golden one. None of the dancers paid me any attention.

Casually I turned my head the other way, keeping the cauldron in my peripheral vision. I saw a pair of male Sidhe approach it, leaning against each other and staggering ever so slightly. They both carried empty cups.

The taller of the pair dipped his cup into the cauldron with great solemnity. I couldn't see from this angle what was in it, but when he raised the cup again, amber liquid was foaming down the side of it. His friend repeated the process, then they both toasted each other and drained their cups dry. I stared, subtlety forgotten, as they did it again, then staggered away, leaning a little more heavily on each other this time.

Beer. They were using the great cauldron of the Dagda, which could provide anything the user's heart desired, to give them beer. I was almost offended. *This* was their big drama? The reason for the desperate struggle to get the damned thing back? Because they wanted free *beer*?

I got up and stalked toward the cauldron, unable to believe it. When I peered into its inky depths I felt a weird sensation, like vertigo. The inside of the cauldron appeared a whole lot bigger than it did from the outside. Just like the TARDIS, only, you know, not blue and able to travel through time. But the cheerful amber liquid that bubbled inside it sure looked and smelled a lot like beer.

"Would you like a drink?" A familiar voice behind me made me jump and spin around, my heart thumping.

The Morrigan offered me a cup, like any good host at a party, though the look on her face wasn't exactly welcoming. She wore her long hair down and twined with flowers. Bare feet peeped out from the hem of her swirling red dress. She looked like the world's scariest hippy. Whatever she wore, there was a chill to her dark eyes that set my teeth on edge and made me long to be anywhere else but here.

"No thanks, I'm underage." No need to let her see how much she unnerved me, though she was probably quite used to having that effect on people.

"The cauldron could make it non-alcoholic for you."

"Nup. I'm good."

She considered me out of those cold dark eyes. "I never expected to see you again."

"Likewise." I straightened my shoulders. "I'd love to say it's a pleasure, but my mother taught me not to lie."

She actually cracked a smile at that. On her face, it wasn't a pleasant expression. A raven cawed and flew down to her shoulder, staring at me from one beady eye. Then it turned its head and gave me the death glare from the other one too. Creepy little freak.

"Did your mother send you here? What exactly do you hope to accomplish in the Sunlit Lands?"

She laid a hand casually on the rim of the cauldron. As if she didn't know! But if she wanted to pretend, I could play along.

"Someone cursed my father. And my friend." She regarded me with polite interest, as if she'd never heard of such a thing. *Was it you, you bitch?* "I want those curses removed."

"When you are older you will learn that we seldom get what we want. If you live that long."

A chill crept down my spine. I was glad I'd sent Zac away, out of her reach. With lightning flashing from her eyes and a storm raging around her she had been terrifying, but this quiet menace was just as scary. She was an ancient goddess of war, with the power to grind me and everyone I cared about into the dust if she felt in the smiting mood.

"These are the people I love." I was determined not to show how afraid I was. "I can't lose them."

Not without a fight, anyway. In my bloodstream the aether fizzed away, reminding me that maybe I could do a little smiting of my own, if it came to that.

"You have still more you can lose," she said.

Did she mean Zac? Fear for him clawed at my heart. But he was safe now, wasn't he, across the sea where she couldn't go?

Or did she mean CJ? "My sister and I are under the protection of Ariel."

Amusement glinted in her dark eyes.

"So you've come to bargain, have you?" The crow wiped its feathered head against her cheek, and she reached up and petted it like a dog. I hoped the stupid bird gave her lice. "You seem an unlikely ambassador."

I shrugged. I'd be a fool to try bargaining with the Sidhe, but it made a good cover story.

"What will you offer to save your world?" she asked.

"My world?" Since when had we been negotiating for the world?

Her turn to shrug. "It was never really yours. It's always been ours. You have only borrowed it for a time." She leaned closer and whispered in my ear. "And now we want it *back*."

I stepped back, repelled by the naked hatred on her face. Instinctively I looked around for CJ. She was still dancing, but a pretty young fairy sat on the bench right next to CJ's backpack. She was watching the dancers too, and seemed unaware of the backpack on the bench next to her. But there was plenty of empty bench. Why sit right there?

The Morrigan still stared at me as if I were a bug she'd like to squash.

"Excuse me," I said, then backed away, desperate to escape that chilling gaze.

I plonked myself down on the other side of the backpack and gave the fairy a hard look. She got up immediately and wandered off. I watched her go, then unbuckled the pack and checked the contents. CJ's rope and compass were still there, and her protein bars and bread roll. The mirror was in a separate compartment, and her water bottle sat in its pocket on the outside. There wasn't much to take anyway, but nothing was missing. Maybe Ariel was right and I was too suspicious, but I was glad that I had the spear in my back pocket, and that my own pack was still firmly on my back.

I looked back, but the Morrigan was gone. I didn't see her among the dancers either. Thank goodness for that. She was one scary fairy. What would the king and queen be like? Like Titania and Oberon from *A Midsummer Night's Dream*? Shakespeare had made them out to be a pair of sex-crazed idiots. Now I wished I'd paid more attention in English last year, though admittedly the toads and diamonds thing had been a little distracting. And Zac. Gorgeous boys with chocolate eyes who flashed cheeky dimples when they smiled were always distracting. The only thing I could remember from the play was the guy called Bottom, and that was only because all the boys developed a terminal case of the sniggers whenever his name came up.

I couldn't help feeling they'd have to be a lot more dangerous than Shakespeare made out, to count the Morrigan as one of their subjects.

CJ came back and collapsed onto the bench.

"God, I'm so thirsty!" She pulled out her drink bottle and took a great long swig.

"Where's Ariel?"

"Gone to tell the royals we're here, I think." She wiped her mouth with the back of her hand. "God, that's good. It's thirsty work out there."

"Well, I'm glad you're not accepting any drinks from him."

She offered me the bottle, but I shook my head. "It's okay, I've still got some of my own." And besides, I hadn't been cavorting around the meadow in the arms of a smarmy Sidhe.

I waited until she was drinking again, then added casually, "By the way, I found the cauldron."

She spat water in surprise and started a coughing fit. "You did? Where?"

I jerked my head. "Over there. They're using it as a beer dispenser."

"Really? Out of all the things they could have used it for?"

"That's what I thought, too." We shared a moment of twin solidarity, and I almost regretted making her inhale her water. Almost. "But at least it's in easy reach."

She frowned at the cauldron for a moment, then looked around at the dancers, and the few onlookers sprawled in the grass, more concerned with their beer than anything else.

"Can it really be that simple? We just take it?"

I must admit, I had that uneasy *it's too good to be true* feeling, too. But for all the stories that told of humans being tricked by the Sidhe, there were plenty of humans outwitting the fairy folk too. They had a great reputation as party animals, and maybe, with the beer flowing, and them feeling secure here in their own world, they really were being as careless as they looked. Perhaps it was arrogance: perhaps they couldn't imagine that anyone could defeat them here, in the heart of their power.

Or maybe the thing was rigged to explode when we touched it, and drown us in beer.

"This might be our best opportunity—while Ariel's gone, and before the king and queen arrive. Who knows what's going to happen then? They think we're here to bargain with them. I don't know how long I can bullshit my way through a negotiation before they figure something's up."

"I don't know." CJ gave me a mocking smile. "I have faith in your bullshitting powers."

"Gee, thanks."

"You're right, though. We should do it before Ariel comes back."

Or the Morrigan. I still felt shaky from our last encounter; I definitely didn't want to meet up with her again. Plus I had the feeling that it might not be so easy to make off with the cauldron under her watchful eye. She didn't strike me as the beer-drinking party animal type.

"So what do we do? Just grab it and make a run for it? Won't they notice?"

"Probably the next time someone comes looking for a drink. But maybe they'll be too drunk to realise we've taken it."

It wasn't much of a plan, but sometimes the simplest ideas are the best. The real problem would be figuring out how to open a gateway home. The mirror had worked before, and with the new magic fizzing around my bloodstream there was a good chance I could get it to work again. But we had to get moving. I couldn't help feeling we were running out of time.

Chapter Seventeen

I cast a last look around the crowds, but no one seemed to be watching us. There was no sign yet of Ariel, either, and that had to be a good thing. He'd stuck pretty close so far. Nor could I see the Morrigan or any of her damn crows.

"Let's do it. I think the coast is clear." Then I caught sight of a familiar face. "No, wait. There's Dewdrop."

The little hedgehog girl lurked under the shadow of the trees at the edge of the meadow, a wistful look on her pointed little face, as if she would have liked to join the festivities but was too shy.

"Where? Is she looking at us?"

"Over there." I nodded in her direction. "Yeah, kind of."

She was watching the dancers, but also keeping an eye on us, casting an anxious glance our way every so often. She caught my eye, and bobbed her head in that nervous way she had.

"You think she's spying on us?"

"Don't know. Don't think so. Hang on—looks like she's coming this way."

The little creature picked her way across the meadow as if expecting something large and toothy to rear out of the ground and take a bite of her. She gave a wide berth to the Sidhe couples lazing on the grass, and nearly jumped out of her prickly skin when a group of goblins went whooping past.

We got up and moved down the long table toward the cauldron. To anyone watching it would look like we were merely going to meet the hedgehog girl.

"Your drink bottle's been leaking." CJ walked behind me, giving her a view of my backpack, which I'd been wearing this whole time. "The whole side of your pack's soaked."

"Really?" I twisted around, half-sliding the pack off my shoulder. Sure enough, the canvas was wet, and the drink bottle completely empty. Further inspection revealed a crack in the plastic at the bottom of the bottle. "Damn. Must have broken it when we fell through the gateway."

And, of course, the minute I knew I had no water I started feeling thirsty. "You got any left?"

"Sure." She held out her bottle to me.

But before I could take it a little furred hand darted between us. "Nonononononono!"

I fell back in shock, and CJ's bottle hit the grass. "Dewdrop! You scared me!"

"No drink," she said firmly.

"It's okay. We brought that water with us." I bent down for the bottle but she kicked it out of reach under the table.

"No drink," she repeated. She waved her hand at the banquet spread on the table before us. "No eat."

"I wasn't going to," I protested. "You're taking this whole guest rite thing very seriously, aren't you?"

I was kind of touched, though. She'd obviously come, even though she was clearly uncomfortable with the crowd, to warn us not to take the Sidhe's magical food. Just because we'd shared a meal, and she felt she owed us the protection of hospitality as a result.

I put an arm round her skinny shoulders, and gently drew her away, back toward the shelter of the trees.

"Why don't we have something to eat together again? I've got some protein bars you're going to love." Over my shoulder I gave CJ a meaningful look, and she nodded. She fell back as I led Dewdrop into the woods.

On a mossy patch, soft as green velvet, I opened my pack and offered Dewdrop one of the protein bars, showing her how to open the wrapper. I had a bread roll left too, but it had gone all soggy in the wet pack. Someone would have to be a lot hungrier than I was to be tempted by that.

Dewdrop bit into the protein bar, and an expression of wonder came over her face.

"Good food!" She broke off a piece and offered it to me, but hedgehog spit wasn't my thing.

"It's okay." I unwrapped another one and took a bite. "I've got one of my own."

We could still hear the music of the fiddle, but it was quieter even this far into the trees. In a moment another sound intruded, a sound I'd been waiting for—my sister rejoining us. I lifted an eyebrow questioningly, not wanting to say anything in front of the hedgehog girl, and CJ nodded, barely able to restrain a triumphant grin. She turned slightly, showing me a bulge in her backpack that hadn't been there before. A nice, cauldron-shaped bulge.

I rose and smiled down at the little hedgehog girl. "It's been lovely meeting you, Dewdrop, but we have to go home now. Our mother will be worried about us. CJ, show her the mirror." We might as well ask, since she was here. Dewdrop drew back as CJ pulled Ariel's mirror from her pack, careful not to show what else was hidden inside. "Do you know how to use this to make a gateway?"

Dewdrop pulled a terrible face, twisting her little whiskered snout almost into a snarl. "Nonono!" She held up one hand as if to shield herself from the mirror. "Watching! Eyes watching."

CJ regarded the mirror uneasily. "Does she mean Ariel can use this to watch us?"

Dewdrop had scrambled to her feet, and was backing slowly across the clearing, her eyes like shiny black buttons, darting from the mirror to our faces and back again.

"I don't know. What did you do to make the gate open before?"

"Nothing. I only used the mirror to talk to Ariel. He opened the gate."

"Put it away then." I was unnerved by the hedgehog girl's reaction. "Or maybe better still, leave it behind. We should go."

CJ held the mirror, still hesitating. A cry rose from the meadow behind us.

"The cauldron!"

This was followed by another sound, which sent chills down my spine: the harsh cawing of many crows, and the thunder of their wings as they all took flight at once.

Looking for us.

"Shit." CJ looked at me, panic in her eyes. "What do we do?"

Dewdrop struck the mirror from CJ's hand. It hit the soft moss and lay glinting darkly. Dewdrop used her toe to turn it over so that the glass faced down, then she flapped her skinny arms at us.

"Go! Go fast!"

We didn't need telling twice. CJ turned and plunged into the trees and I followed close behind. Yet I knew, however fast we ran, it wouldn't be fast enough to outrun the Morrigan's little pets. And if Ariel had already seen where we were because of that stupid mirror, we were pretty much screwed. Running wasn't going to help.

"Stop!" I snatched at the back of CJ's pack to slow her down. "We can't outrun them."

She turned a frightened face to me. "Then what do we do? The cauldron?"

"Won't work," I said. Maybe that was why it had been so easy to steal—because the Sidhe knew we couldn't use it to escape. "I have a better idea."

"Make it snappy." She glanced back the way we'd come, where voices called to each other beneath the trees.

I pulled the spear from my back pocket and gave it a new shape: an old-fashioned key, big as my hand, with an ornate filigree head.

"Nice," said CJ, "but where's the lock?"

"Give me a minute."

My heart was pounding, and not just from the run. I tried to block out the sounds of pursuit, and CJ's worried face urging me to hurry, but I was no Zen master. I shut my eyes, clutching the new key so hard it dug into my hand, and thought of home.

Throw your heart at it, Puck's voice whispered in my mind.

I thought of Mum. God, she was going to be mad at us, but how I wished she was here now. I thought of Sona, lying in that bed, needing help so desperately, and Sergei, sad and hurting. Zac with his dimples and his warm brown eyes. I longed for home with all my heart: the people that made up my home, my family. Mum, Sona and Zac, the warders, even annoying Dorian, plus Simon and the twins, Ronnie and Gretel.

But most of all Dad. I needed to get back to him, needed to *help* him, so badly. I missed my Dad, my own stupid joke-telling, annoying know-it-all of a father. I missed his hugs and his loud whistling; I missed his sudden enthusiasms and his crazy ideas. I wanted him back.

I heard a soft intake of breath from CJ and opened my eyes to see pink light streaming from the key. It formed a shape that grew in the air before us—the shape of a door.

"Hurry up!" CJ begged.

The noises of pursuit were getting louder. Voices shouted through the woods behind us, and a sudden flapping overhead brought the first crow to perch on a branch above us. It cawed loudly, and soon half a dozen of its mates joined it. CJ picked up a stick and threw it at them, but they only lifted briefly into the air, then resettled on the branch.

"Going as fast as I can," I said through gritted teeth, though, to be honest, I had no real idea what I was doing, or if it was even possible to control the speed at which I was doing it. The feel of aether fizzing through me and into the key, and vice versa, was like tiny bubbles bursting all over my skin. I didn't dare take my eyes from the doorway in case it all somehow collapsed.

A shining pink keyhole appeared on my magical glowing door. The trees behind it were still visible, tinted pink through its translucence.

"Go on!" CJ urged. "Put the key in."

I thrust the key into the insubstantial lock and turned it. There was a faint click, and the door fell away from my hand, revealing our bedroom in the guest quarters at headquarters, with CJ's dirty clothes strewn across the floor.

I'd never been so glad to see a pair of CJ's dirty undies in my life.

"Hurry up! I don't know how long this thing will hold."

I strode forward, feeling a faint shudder through my body as I crossed the magical threshold.

"How did you do that?"

I looked back to find CJ fighting her way forward, bent over as if she struggled headfirst into a gale-force wind.

"I just walked through. What the hell are you doing?" Behind her I saw flashes of colour through the trees. The hunt was very close. "Hurry up!"

"I'm not doing this on purpose!" she snapped. "It feels like something's pushing me away."

She forced her foot one step closer, her face bright red with effort.

I darted back out. "Is it the cauldron? Give me your pack."

She wrestled her pack off and I hurled it through the door. There was a heavy clunk as the cauldron banged hard against the far wall.

She shook her head, a panicked look in her eyes. "It makes no difference."

I grabbed her hand. "Let me help you."

With me pulling she made better progress, but it felt as if I was dragging a block of concrete across the forest floor. I started to panic. We weren't going to make it in time.

Maybe I could bring the doorway closer? I glanced back at it, but I was too panicked now to throw my heart at it. The damn thing was just about pounding its way out of my chest.

I stretched out my free arm and found the edge of the doorway. It looked insubstantial, but it felt solid enough under my fingers. Though I felt like I was tearing myself in half, I managed to drag CJ right to the brink.

"You'll never get her through there, you know," said a familiar cold voice, "no matter how hard you pull. She has drunk of our waters, and may never leave."

CJ screamed as the Morrigan loomed behind her. Her hand slipped from mine and I fell back through the doorway. I sprawled on the bedroom floor among my sister's clothes, my last sight of her the look of despair on her face as the Morrigan dragged her away.

The door snapped shut, leaving no sign it had ever existed.

"CJ!"

I scrabbled on the floor for the key, which had fallen among the clothes when the door winked out of existence. Then I shut my eyes and longed for CJ with all the desperation and fear I could manage. And believe me, it was a lot.

But I didn't feel that fizz in the blood, the popping and tickling I'd come to associate with aether at work. I knew before I opened my eyes that it hadn't worked.

I sank down on my bed and stared at the key in my hand. It was totally drained. Maybe if it spent the night in the vault …

No. Who was I kidding? It had only worked in Tir na nÓg because the whole place was just one big ball of aether. Because when I was there, *I* was filled with aether, and somehow, through the spear, I could access the power that in this world was only latent. If it was that easy to open a gate from this side, wouldn't someone have done it before now? But what was the alternative? I couldn't just give up. My sister was trapped there, and I had to find a way to get her back.

The Morrigan's last words rang in my ears. *She has drunk of our waters, and may never leave.* What was she talking about? When had CJ ever drunk anything of theirs? She'd only drunk from her own bottle.

And then I remembered the fairy, sitting so nonchalantly next to CJ's backpack, when the whole rest of the bench was free. I'd been worried that she'd been taking something *out* of CJ's pack, but I'd had it all wrong. She'd been putting something *in*. While that bitch the Morrigan had distracted me, the fairy had switched CJ's safe water for some of theirs.

And now she was trapped there because of it. If Dewdrop hadn't stopped me drinking it, I would be too.

But surely not forever, whatever the Morrigan said? There must be a way to get her back. Mum would know. I shoved the key into my pocket and raced out into the corridor in search of her.

What time was it? My watch had stopped at 6:52. That must have been when we left our world that morning. Was it only that morning? A sudden terrible fear seized me—that years had gone by—and I pounded down the fire stairs in search of someone. Anyone.

Gretel was the first person I saw.

"Gretel! What day is it?"

"The day you get your arse kicked." The last time I'd seen such a fierce look on her face she'd been condensing the Morrigan. "What the hell have you two been up to? The whole place is in an uproar because of that stunt you pulled this morning."

Thank God. I sagged against her. "So it was only this morning?"

"Ye gods and little fishes. You really did pass through, didn't you?" She stared at me, the fierceness replaced by wonder. "I could hardly believe it when Simon and Kyle came back with some story about pink flashes and disappearing girls. Your poor mother's had half the seekers out combing the streets for you all day."

"Where is Mum? I have to talk to her."

"She's not here. She had to fly out to Townsville."

Wow. Now it was my turn to stare. Her daughters were missing and she still flew out?

Gretel correctly interpreted the look on my face. "Did you forget about the re-anchoring ceremony? It's tonight. They had to go ahead regardless."

"But they didn't have the cauldron. Or the spear."

Gretel's eyebrows flew up. "How did you know about the

spear? Don't tell me *you* took it." When I said nothing, she groaned. "You did, didn't you? I can't believe it. What is the *matter* with you? You put this whole operation at risk! For what?"

"It was CJ, actually. Who took it, I mean. Oh, what does it matter what for? Here, have it back."

I slapped the key into her hand, and she stared, dumbfounded. "*That's* the spear of Lugh?"

"Yes, but look, they can't go ahead with the ceremony."

Gretel was still staring at the key, turning it over in her hands as if afraid it might explode. "Why not?"

"Because CJ's there. She's still in Tir na nÓg. She's trapped, and if they close off the leaks now, we'll never get her back." Fear dug its sharp claws into my heart. Saying it made it seem too real.

Gretel's head came up sharply. "What do you mean, she's trapped?"

I started to give her the condensed version of what happened, but before I'd got any further than meeting Ariel, she'd taken my elbow and started marching me down the corridor.

"Where are we going?"

"The warders need to hear this."

We found Dorian and Dena in the library, surrounded by books that looked like they'd come from the restricted section. As the door opened, Dorian looked up, impatience at the interruption on his face, but his expression changed when he recognised me.

He shut his book with a thud that made Dena jump. "You're back. You have a lot of explaining to do, young lady."

"That's why I brought her, sir," said Gretel.

"Thank you, Gretel," Dena said. "You may go."

Gretel shoved the key at me and disappeared, leaving me to face the glares of the two warders alone. I rushed through an explanation of what had happened, from CJ stealing the spear this morning, through Ariel's opening of the gate through the mirror, meeting the Morrigan again and the switcheroo with the water, to the last terrible moments in the forest when I'd opened a door back to our world but CJ had been unable to pass through.

"And there's the spear back," I said, stepping forward to lay the key on top of his closed book.

He stared at it for a long moment, his finger tracing the design. When he looked up his face was bleak.

"I can see we will have a lot to talk about in the coming days. But for the moment we will have to set aside your incredible effrontery in taking the spear into danger until after the evening's ceremonies are concluded." He looked at Dena and sighed heavily. "I don't look forward to telling Jane that her daughter is trapped in Tir na nÓg."

Dena glared at me as if I'd trapped CJ there on purpose. "I thought you, at least, had more common sense. That was a terrible risk you took. I suppose we must think ourselves lucky that we have only lost Crystal. It could have been so much worse."

"Wait." The finality of their talk sent chills down my spine. "There must still be a way to get her back, right? Some way to open another gate?"

Dorian shook his head, his face grave. "Sadly, Violet, in life we don't always get a second chance, as you will learn as you get older. No opportunity to fix our mistakes. All we can do is learn from them."

"But we can't … we can't just *leave* her there." I could hear my voice creeping higher, and hated how whiny it made me sound, but it was all I could do not to cry. "We could use the spear, like I did before …"

"There is no time," Dena said gently. "We must perform the ceremony tonight. There is no more time left."

Funny, that wasn't the tune she'd been singing before CJ and I left. "What happened to *we might have months yet before the walls fail?* You were arguing against this ceremony just the other day."

"You happened. You and your sister disappeared into Tir na nÓg, showing us how completely the Sidhe have infiltrated our organisation, and how close they are to breaking out forever. Whatever you did to smash through the wall has all but brought it down."

"So you're saying it's *my* fault that you're going ahead with this ceremony?" Horror stole my breath away. In trying to save Dad, and Sona—and even poor bloody Sergei, who meant nothing to me—CJ and I had convinced the warders of the urgency of the Sidhe threat. My own mother had decided the risk was so great she was prepared to sacrifice both her daughters to save the world from the Sidhe. How cold would you have to be to make a decision like that? I just couldn't make that fit with the soft, loving mother I knew.

Or thought I knew.

"But you can't," I whispered. "CJ's in there. We have to at least try to get her out."

Dorian shook his head. "I'm sorry, Violet. I know what it is like to lose someone you love. I would help you if I could, but there is nothing to be done. If she drank while she was there, I'm afraid the Morrigan was right. She's trapped there forever."

"I'll ring Mum." I threw my shoulders back and forced myself to look them in the eye. "She won't let you go ahead when she knows CJ's still inside."

Dena came around the table and took my hands in hers. "Honey, I'm truly sorry, but your mother knows what's at stake. She will be overjoyed to hear you've returned safely, but her answer will be the same as ours."

"No! You're wrong." I stormed out, slamming the door behind me.

But once in the corridor, I ran out of defiance and slid slowly down the wall to the carpet, like a rag doll that had lost its stuffing. Mum had been prepared to seal up the Sidhe prison when she thought *both* of us were inside. Knowing that CJ was still there wouldn't make any difference.

I put my head down on my knees and cried.

Chapter Eighteen

I wasn't exactly sent to my room in disgrace, but Dorian made it quite clear that my presence wasn't required any further.

That suited me fine. I wanted no part of their stupid ceremony. I'd rung Mum, but she wasn't answering her phone, probably too caught up in preparations of her own. She had the sword in Townsville, and Frida had the stone in Perth. Bryan was in Broome covering the last of the four compass points but of course, since we'd taken the spear before he'd set out, he had no treasure to call on for power. Instead Dorian and Dena had sent Sergei with him, hoping Bryan would be able to draw on the aether that fuelled the ogre's curse. They'd been planning to use Sona the same way here in Sydney until I reappeared with both the spear and the cauldron. Now Kyle was winging his way to Broome on a private jet, hoping to arrive in time with the spear, and the cauldron was set to take on the starring role in the Sydney ceremony.

I lay on my bed and stared at the ceiling. There were no lights on, but I could still make out the shapes of CJ's clothes on the floor, and the clutter of her bits and pieces on the chest of drawers between our two beds. I missed her with a fierce ache; like losing a limb, the space where she used to be throbbed with pain. Half the time she drove me crazy, and we fought like—well, like most sisters, I guess. That didn't mean that I didn't love her. She was a part of me. Sure, we'd spent time apart before, for sleepovers or camps. But this was different. I just couldn't fathom that I might never see her again.

The worst part was knowing there was nothing I could do. At least before, we'd had a plan—and, okay, it had all gone horribly wrong in the end, but we'd *tried*. We'd been doing something, trying to fix the problems that nobody else seemed to want to face up to. Now I was helpless, and the useless waiting was killing me.

Actually, no, scratch that. The worst part was knowing it was my fault. If CJ and I hadn't run off with the spear to fairyland, the warders might still be umming and aahing over their ceremony, instead of prancing around in the dark right now on top of Observatory Hill, desperately trying to put an end to any hope of ever getting CJ back. Had this been the Sidhe's plan all along? Was that why the cauldron had been set up so temptingly as bait? But what did they gain by trapping CJ in fairyland forever?

My nose was blocked and my head throbbed from all the tears I'd shed, but I sat up and swung my feet onto the floor. I couldn't just lie here in the dark. If it really was my fault that the warders were pushing ahead with the ceremony so fast, then I simply had to find a way to stop them. CJ had no one else to fight for her. It was up to me.

I eased open the door of the guest quarters and peeked out into the corridor. No one around. They were probably all up on Observatory Hill, capering widdershins round the statue of Hans Christian Andersen or whatever their stupid ritual required. Just as long as they all kept their clothes on. Dorian Kincumber naked was something I never wanted to see. I hadn't paid much attention to the details of the ceremony, but hopefully it didn't involve naked capering. Whatever. My focus was on making sure it didn't go ahead.

There was no one around, and my sneakers made no noise as I slipped through the dark corridors. The ping of the lift made me jump. It sounded very loud in the stillness, and I imagined hordes of cranky people swarming the corridors to find out what I was up to, but the place was like a ghost town. Next thing a tumbleweed would roll past for sure.

I finally found someone when I opened the door to Dad's accommodation. Emmet was engrossed in something on his iPad, and jumped as I squeezed into the little anteroom.

"What are you doing here?" he asked. "It's nearly eleven-thirty. Shouldn't you be asleep or something?"

"I'm seventeen, Emmet, not three." Did he really think I could sleep while all his mates did their best to trap my sister in fairyland forever? "I thought I'd come down and see Dad."

"He's not asleep either. He seems anxious, for some reason. He's been pacing a lot."

I peered through the glass panel on the door into the main room, and saw the big polar bear moving along the far wall. The blinds above him were open, and his white fur glinted in the moonlight. When he reached the corner he swung his massive head round and lumbered back the other way.

"Do you want me to come in?" Emmet gestured at the dart gun that rested against the wall. "In case he's not feeling in a friendly mood?"

Having someone with a gun accompany me, even if it was only a tranquilliser gun, probably wouldn't make Dad feel any friendlier. I opened the door. "No, thanks."

Dad stopped mid-pace, one huge paw lifted like a question mark, and regarded me in silence. His dark eyes glittered oddly.

"Dad?" I moved forward slowly, careful not to make any sudden moves, and kept my voice calm and low. It had been a while since my last visit. Would he even recognise me? "It's me, Violet."

He made a snuffling noise, and a pink tongue flicked out and licked his black nose. The big bear ears pricked forward as if he was listening, so I kept going. Hopefully tonight would be one of his more lucid times. The fact that he was awake and pacing was a good sign. Maybe he could sense that something was going on.

"We've got a problem. CJ's in trouble, and we need your help."

He padded toward me. I stood my ground, though it took an effort. You don't appreciate just how big polar bears are until you're standing toe to toe with one. He could crush me with one blow if he wanted to.

He lowered his big head and rubbed it against me affectionately. Even that was enough to make me stagger, but I was so relieved he knew me, I didn't care. I threw my arms around his neck.

"What do you say we go for a little walk together?"

He made a snorting noise that could have meant anything, but I decided to take it as agreement.

"Great. Let's go."

If it was half past eleven we should have plenty of time. The ceremony was due to culminate at midnight, Sydney time. I'd taken in that much of the planning, at least. The other sites were performing theirs simultaneously, though obviously it wouldn't be midnight at those. Perth and Broome were three hours behind us, and Townsville was one. I'd gathered that midnight was considered the optimal time for some reason, but I didn't know what made Sydney's midnight better than anyone else's. Maybe because this had been the main site for the original anchoring.

Whatever. Observatory Hill was less than five minutes' walk away, so we should have enough time to well and truly screw up the ceremony before it could be completed. I was guessing most magic rituals wouldn't survive having a polar bear trample through them. With a bit of luck, they'd be so distracted by Dad I'd have a chance to snatch the cauldron, and then they'd be back to square one.

"Stay close, now," I warned him.

He rumbled at me: polar bear indigestion or agreement? Who knew? I opened the door and he surged through, his big shoulders brushing the doorway on each side.

Emmet leapt to his feet. "Oh, shit, you let him out."

He made a half-hearted attempt to go for the tranq gun, but Dad was in the way. It was a small room anyway, and Dad took up most of it. Emmet pressed himself back against the wall, his eyes behind their dark-rimmed spectacles huge with fear as Dad's massive head swung round to stare at him. I nabbed the gun myself and waved it in Emmet's general direction. Like CJ had said: how hard could it be? In America even kids could do it.

"Violet, what the *hell* are you doing?" he whispered out the side of his mouth, obviously trying not to draw Dad's attention.

I gestured with the gun. "Get inside, Emmet."

Emmet went, and I shut the door and locked him in.

"You can't take him outside." Emmet pressed up against the glass panel in the door, his voice muffled. "Anything could happen."

Ignoring him, I peeked out into the corridor. All clear. Dad and I bolted for the front door. Well, I bolted. Dad kept it to a gentle lumber, but that was fast enough to keep up with me.

The automatic doors were locked for the night, but I pressed the release button and they slid open. Dad shied a little at the movement, then propped on the pavement outside, sniffing doubtfully at the warm night air. I suppose to a polar bear a big city like Sydney must smell pretty strange.

"Come on, Dad." I closed my fist on a big hunk of hair and urged him on, but tugging a polar bear is a waste of time when you only weigh fifty kilos. He wouldn't move unless he wanted to. "This way. Please! We've got to go. The Sidhe have got CJ."

I looked back anxiously, but there were no signs of pursuit yet. That might not last long. After a pause that felt like forever Dad decided he'd had enough of sniffing and followed me down the street, while I quickly filled him in on the situation. I don't know how much, if any, he understood, but he seemed to be paying attention. That gave me hope.

I chose the most direct route to the Observatory, forgetting, until we went round the corner, that it took us past one of the busiest and most popular pubs in The Rocks.

I pulled up short at the sight of drinkers spilling out onto the pavement, all having a raucous good time.

"Oh, shit."

That was nothing to what *they* said when they saw the bear.

"Quick, Dad. Back this way!"

Dad followed as the screams and cries of amazement mounted behind us. So did a few of the drinkers. I mean, seriously. Who does that? Wouldn't any normal person run the *other* way when they saw a polar bear loose on the streets? What did they think they were going to do if they caught up? A couple of them brandished pool cues as if they might try bludgeoning the bear to death with them. They seemed to be under the impression they were rescuing me from him, from what I could tell from their drunken cries. They must have been seriously hammered.

We ducked down an alley to try to shake them off. It was kind of hard to hide something as big as a polar bear, though. Most of them ran past, but one stopped at the mouth of the alley and peered doubtfully into the darkness. Maybe he wasn't as drunk as his friends, but he was still stupid, because he started to sneak down that alley like some kind of bear-slaying ninja.

Dad growled. Crouched in the dark of an alley in the middle of the night, that sound was bloodcurdling enough to raise the hairs on *my* arms, let alone ninja guy's. He yelped and fled back toward the light.

"Down here, guys!"

I ran to the far end of the alley. Dad knocked over something that clanged so loudly every dog in a ten-kilometre radius started barking. I led him down little streets and round corners. The

Rocks is full of little hidey-holes and strange little passageways. We toured quite a few of them, trying to shake off pursuit.

At one stage I heard the wail of a police siren approaching. I sure hoped that was for someone else, and not in response to panicked calls about a wild animal loose in the city. We found a quiet spot in an alley behind a bread shop and hunkered down, waiting for all the attention to die away.

I crouched next to Dad, his fur tickling my arm, and sucked in big lungfuls of air. I hadn't run like that in ages, and all that ducking and weaving had eaten into our precious time. Now it was a quarter to twelve. We couldn't afford to wait here much longer.

At ten to, I decided we had to risk it. I hadn't heard any shouts for a while. We edged out of our hiding place into a quiet street that was mainly residential. Closer to the Observatory the streets would be wider and more open. Probably with lots more people too, even at this time of night. Maybe I'd underestimated the difficulty of sneaking a polar bear through a major capital city.

We made it as far as Argyle Street without being spotted. Luckily it was only by a guy and girl walking arm-in-arm. Though the girl screamed, they showed no desire to chase us. Very sensible of them. Running up the slope to Observatory Hill, we scattered a larger group that looked like a hen's night out. One girl was wearing a fluffy pink tiara. There was a lot of squealing, and they stopped to watch us run past. A couple of them even whipped out their mobile phones and started filming. Great. Another starring role on YouTube for yours truly. But at least they didn't totter after us on their high heels.

I was so relieved to reach the relative safety of the little park by the Observatory I almost forgot that the hard part was still to come. I remembered abruptly when Simon stepped out of the dark and caught my arm.

"What are you doing here?"

I pulled, but he had no intention of letting go. "We have to stop them, Simon!"

"We? Who's w—bloody hell!" He leapt back and drew his gun as Dad loomed behind me.

"No! Don't shoot!" I tried to shield Dad, but there was way too much bear and not enough girl to do the job. Our yells attracted more seekers, who soon had us surrounded. Dad growled, a continuous ominous rumbling in my ear. His big head swung around the circle, eyeing each seeker in turn, as if trying to decide which one to eat first. A couple of them shifted nervously.

Nervous men with guns. Not a good combination.

"What the hell are you playing at, Violet?" Simon didn't take his eyes off Dad, and his gun never wavered. "Why did you bring him here?"

"And how are we going to get him back?" one of the other guys muttered.

"Simon, please!" Over by the fence, where the leak was strongest—where CJ and I had entered Ariel's gateway—Dorian stood over the cauldron chanting. He held a portable condensor, and three large condensors on stands, like the ones Gretel had used last year to save me from the Morrigan, were set up in a triangle around him. Dena stood beside him, and a faint pink glow surrounded them. A hint of burnt toffee drifted on the air.

"Let us through. They can't do this. We've got to at least *try* to save CJ first."

The condensor in Dorian's hands suddenly lit up like a hot pink Christmas tree and the smell of burnt toffee washed over me, much stronger than before. The light was so bright it was as if someone had just shone a torch right in my face, and I threw up a hand to protect my dazzled eyes.

"We can't do that, Violet. I'm sorry. Now take your dad and move away, please."

Some of the other seekers murmured, distracted by the bright light. The big condensors started to whine, a high-pitched, unpleasant noise like a jet engine winding up for take-off— though not as loud, thank God, or we would have had the police down on us any moment.

Actually, maybe I should be hoping for that. One look at what was going on here and any self-respecting policeman would be arresting the lot of them just in case.

"I'll scream. I'll yell 'fire!' until the cops turn up."

A look of distaste crossed his face. "For God's sake, Violet, it's not all about you. Surely you wouldn't risk the safety of the whole world just to get your own way?"

Dad's growling increased in volume, as if he understood Simon's words. Maybe the aether here was affecting him. He shifted against me and I looked up, getting a faceful of hot fishy breath. But he wasn't looking at Simon, or me. His gaze was trained on Dorian, and the increasingly bright glow surrounding him and Dena.

Now I could see pink mist twining around the railings of the fence and creeping across the grass. As I watched, a whole slithery pink mess started to coalesce into something that looked remarkably like the rent that we had fallen through into fairyland.

"I think the safety of the whole world could be in trouble anyway. Look at that."

"Nice try." Simon's gaze never moved from Dad. Behind him Dena suddenly tried to snatch the condensor from Dorian's hands, and he shoved her roughly away.

"No, really, Simon. Look!" A couple of the other seekers had turned away, transfixed by the bright glow. My nostrils twitched as a blast of burnt toffee hit them, stronger than I'd ever smelled before. At least in this world.

"Dorian, stop!" I yelled. "You're letting more aether in. It's all going wrong!"

The whine of the condensors was becoming painful. Dena lunged again, and Dorian struck her across the face. She collapsed in a heap at his feet. Dorian glanced over at me, his head wreathed in pink flame. His face was alight with excitement.

"No, it's all going right," he shouted. "At last!"

Pink light burst from the cauldron, lancing into the sky like a searchlight. My ears popped as if the pressure had suddenly changed, and pink washed across the sky in a giant wave.

While we all stood goggling at the stars, Dad surged forward, catching even Simon unawares. Simon's gun barked, but Dad mowed him down and kept on going.

I screamed and ran after Dad. Dorian saw us coming and started yelling at the seekers, but no one could hear him over the roar that was coming from the cauldron as aether fountained into the glowing sky. Most of them weren't even looking at him.

And then a black bird darted out of the light, followed by another, and another, until the night sky was thick with them, and their harsh cries competed with the thunder of aether exploding back into the world. That stirred the seekers into movement, though their guns were little use against the barrage of birds that swooped and slashed at them. Simon charged at Dorian, but couldn't break through the magic barrier protecting him.

I ducked and covered my head with my arms, screaming abuse at the feathered nightmares that dived on me out of the dark. Only Dorian, and Dena on the ground at his feet, remained unaffected in their glowing pink bubble.

"Enough!" A voice rolled across the sky like thunder, and the crows and ravens settled wherever they could find a roost. They lined the top of the fence around the Observatory in beady-eyed black, shuffling and rustling.

The Morrigan stepped out of the pink light and smiled at Dorian. "Well done."

I stared at Dorian in horror. He'd done this on purpose? Many more shapes moved behind the Morrigan in the pink light. A whole army of Sidhe waited, ready for their first taste of freedom.

He gave her a courtly bow, and I wanted to punch his smiling, traitorous face. But before I could move, Dad roared into action. The Morrigan stood calmly in his path. She raised her hand.

"No!" I screamed.

Her magic hit him mid-leap. The polar bear twisted in the air, and a naked man fell to the ground at her feet.

Chapter Nineteen

"Hello, Douglas."

Dad groaned. I rushed to him and dropped to my knees on the grass. His skin—his smooth, human skin—was warm to the touch as I grabbed his shoulder.

"Dad!" God, it was so good to see him.

He opened his eyes and blinked up at me. His blue eyes looked almost purple in the pink glow surrounding us. "Hey, love." He looked around, frowning. "I just had the weirdest dream."

The Morrigan laughed. For a moment I'd forgotten she was there, forgotten the whole terrible mess in the excitement of seeing Dad back. Why had she changed him back? I'd thought she meant to kill him.

"That was no dream," she said. "You made a good bear, but I must say, I prefer you in this form. Although …" She flicked her hand as if waving away a fly, and a pair of shorts and a T-shirt with the words "Morrigan Rocks" blazoned across it appeared on his naked body. "You look better with clothes on."

Dad struggled into a sitting position, and I helped him stand. She smiled at him.

"You see, we can be generous in triumph. There is no need for our peoples to be at war."

"You mean you'll leave us alone?" Dena said. Dad looked too dazed still to speak.

"Speaking for myself, of course. I am the chooser of the slain, not the slayer." Her long black hair billowed in the wind as aether rushed around her. She smiled. It wasn't a pleasant expression. "Unfortunately, I cannot speak for all my people. Some of them feel they are owed somewhat for two centuries of imprisonment."

She swept one arm wide in a dramatic gesture, and a horde of Sidhe emerged from the mists behind her. Some were as beautiful as she, and rode in a stately procession, their horses garlanded with flowers. Their mounts' hooves made little sound when they hit the asphalt of the street beyond us. Guess there were no iron horseshoes there.

The women wore dresses in bright colours, all soft shining silks and floaty fabrics. Their hair was long and braided. So was the men's, but they wore pants and full-sleeved shirts. Just as well. Half of them were so pretty they could easily have been mistaken for girls.

Other Sidhe weren't so easy on the eye. I watched open-mouthed as bat-winged creatures with fanged faces launched into the Sydney skies and misshapen figures that looked like walking piles of rags shambled out of the pink mists. Small creatures with oddly-formed legs hopped or lurched among the horses' hooves, and shy fox-faced ones scurried past. I looked for Dewdrop but didn't see her.

Nor was another longed-for face among the laughing, chattering crowds. Where was CJ? Surely if the Sidhe could leave their prison, she could too?

"My lady." Dorian stepped forward and bowed. "I hate to press you, but … my reward?"

"Ah, yes. Your wife." Her dark gaze fell on his eager face. "How is she?"

Some of the light faded from his eyes. "She's failing fast, my lady. I must hurry."

"Give me your hands then. Never let it be said that the Morrigan does not keep her promises."

He thrust his hands out and she clasped them between her own. A rosy glow flared, then died away.

"Go," she said. "You have the power of healing, until the moon rises again. Use it well."

He nodded and turned away. His eyes caught Dad's for a moment, then dropped under the weight of accusation there.

"I'm sorry," he muttered, then he hurried away.

I watched him go, still reeling. All along, Dorian had been the traitor. No wonder no one had been able to find out who it was. The warders themselves had been above suspicion. He'd orchestrated this whole thing. He'd always been the one pushing to re-enact the anchoring ceremony. And all along, he'd meant to subvert it and release the Sidhe instead. All to save one woman.

No one moved to stop him. In fact, no one moved at all as the Sidhe continued to pour out of their former prison. What was the point? None of us had the power to stand up to that. Every person I could see stood with shoulders slumped, watching the end of everything they had fought for.

Still the Morrigan lingered, as if waiting for something, so we waited too, frozen to the spot in all our useless horror. I scanned each face that emerged from the mists, hope the only thing still keeping me on my feet. I longed for CJ with every fibre of my being, but I felt no tickle of aether in my veins. For all the aether that was pouring into the world, it seemed that none of it was entering me. Magic had seemed so easy in Tir na nÓg, as if all I needed was enough aether and a burning desire. But there must be more to it.

Maybe if I used the cauldron? But the Morrigan was standing right there, not three steps from it. She wasn't going to stand back and let me use it, if I even could. So I kept watching the crowd, hoping and praying to see a familiar sleek dark head and a pair of bright blue eyes.

The flood of Sidhe had slowed to a trickle when a last shining pair emerged, mounted on identical horses, so white they gleamed silver in the moonlight. One was a woman even more beautiful than all the beauties who'd already passed, with a golden circlet nestled in her dark hair. Her companion had dark hair too, though his was streaked with silver. He was the first Sidhe I'd seen who didn't look like a twenty-year-old, and I didn't need to see the crown on his head to realise I was looking at the king and queen of the Sidhe.

The Morrigan bowed gracefully. "Your Majesties."

The king looked down on her and smiled. "You've done well, Morrigan."

The Morrigan's smile turned smug. "I promised you freedom, and I delivered it."

"Indeed. We are most pleased." His gaze swept over the park, taking in the Observatory, the road, and the dark city hulking behind it. From here we could see all the way across the harbour to North Sydney, with the curve of the Harbour Bridge glowing softly in the foreground. His lip curled. "Although it seems the world has not improved in our absence."

"So much iron," the queen said softly.

"I daresay you will still find much to please you, sire," said the Morrigan.

"You are right." The king smiled, and the effect was dazzling. "Will you ride with us, Morrigan?"

"It would be my pleasure."

A bent little man with skin so rough it looked more like bark led forward a great black horse. The horse's eyes shone red, as if it were possessed. A trick of the light or something more? I shuddered. It seemed fitting for the Morrigan.

The black horse stamped its feet and tossed its head so sharply the little man was lifted from his feet. He squealed in surprise, which only spooked the horse more. It stamped and snorted, and while everyone's eyes were on it, I sidled closer to the cauldron.

Everyone said there was no escape from fairyland for CJ, and the fact that she hadn't appeared even as their prison emptied of Sidhe seemed to confirm that. But it was also a fact that the great cauldron of the Dagda could produce a lot more than beer. Anything you wished for could be pulled from its inky depths.

So which would win in a battle of the magics? Would they cancel each other out? Or could the cauldron, one of the four great treasures of the Sidhe, produce my heart's desire in defiance of the laws of Tir na nÓg?

Only one way to find out.

With CJ in my heart and a prayer on my lips, I plunged my hand into the cauldron. The king of the Sidhe was laughing at the little man swinging on the end of the horse's halter, despite said little man's imminent danger of being trampled by the restless hooves of the horse. His queen and the Morrigan watched too. No one was looking at me as I bent over the cauldron, squinting against the glare of the aether that still poured from it.

My heart hammered with fear and desperation as I groped in the bottom of the cauldron. *Please, please, please.* I needed CJ so much. I'd rather spend the rest of my life trapped in fairyland, too, than stay here without her. I shut my eyes and focused all my longing on my sister. What was apple pie without cream? Or Laurel without Hardy? Ceej was the Jekyll to my Hyde—or was it the other way around? You couldn't have one without the other. We were a part of the same whole.

My searching fingers met resistance, and I pushed. *Come on, Ceej. Where are you?* Something brushed against my fingers and I jumped. But this was no time for hesitation. I shoved my hand back down.

And found another one.

Oh, my God. I plunged my other arm in too and got a good grip on that hand. It clung to mine and I pulled with everything I had.

The king stopped laughing. "What is she doing?"

His voice had an urgency that snapped the Morrigan's head around. She raised a hand and Dad lunged to intercept her.

Joy swept through me as my sister's arm emerged from the cauldron. Somehow that dinky little pot expanded, and first her head appeared, followed by her shoulders. My arms strained with effort as our eyes met, but there was no way I was letting her go. The Morrigan could send all her ravens against me, I didn't care.

Someone screamed, in warning or protest. CJ slithered out of the cauldron like a newborn baby, smeared in aether, and we tumbled on the grass together.

And then there was an almighty explosion as the great cauldron of the Dagda shattered into a million pieces.

Chapter Twenty

I don't remember much of the rest of that night. My ears rang, and my arms ran with blood from a dozen tiny cuts. Luckily the force of the blast was away from us, or we both could have been cut to ribbons. I think I blacked out for a while there. All I remember is holding CJ, and Dad crying and asking us over and over again if we were all right.

There was a lot of shouting but it all sounded like it was happening at the other end of a very long tunnel. I remember hoping that my hearing hadn't been permanently damaged, and a confused impression of being jostled in someone's arms as they carried me away.

And then I woke up, and it was morning, and Dad was sitting by my bed, looking exhausted but blissfully human.

"Where's CJ?" I asked.

He grinned. "Typical. No 'good morning, darling Daddy'. Just 'where's CJ?' Guess I'm not the favourite after all."

I jumped out of bed and threw my arms around him. He hugged me back, hard, and I breathed in his familiar smell with relief. My Dad was back.

"Good morning, darling Daddy." I rubbed his stubbly chin. "You need a shave."

He grinned and ran a hand over his face. "What are you talking about? This is the least amount of facial hair I've had in months."

"Some of us are trying to sleep, you know," said a grumpy voice, "but *someone* keeps talking."

We were in our own bedroom in the guest quarters, and CJ was sprawled in the other bed, pretending to scowl at me. Right back where she belonged.

"Hey," I said. She looked good. Better than good. She looked absolutely perfect; not a mark on her.

"Hey, yourself," she said. A smile peeked out and she gave up trying to look grumpy. "That was pretty smart thinking last night. I'm impressed."

"Shame you had to destroy the cauldron in the process," Dad said, "but I guess it was a worthy cause. I'm quite attached to the idea of having *two* daughters."

"Yeah, me too. I don't know what happened there. Why did the cauldron explode?"

Dad shrugged. "I think you created a bit of a magical conundrum. The cauldron's magic wanted to give you CJ, but the laws of Tir na nÓg said she couldn't leave. The two opposing magics got into a bit of an arm wrestle and the cauldron just couldn't take the pressure."

"A magical arm wrestle?" CJ said. "That's pretty technical talk, Dad. Are you sure you couldn't explain it more simply?"

"Don't be so critical. I've still got bear brain. It's a wonder I can form sentences at all."

"I thought I remembered getting hurt last night," I said, twisting my arm around to check it. The skin was unblemished all over.

"You did," Dad said. "You should have seen CJ's back. It took us half an hour to pick all the little bits of cauldron out of it. But Dorian used his healing power on both of you."

A shadow crossed his face at Dorian's name. I stared in surprise.

"He came back?" I'd been under the impression we were never going to see him again. He'd got what he wanted—the power to heal his dying wife—and there'd be no welcome for him among the warders any more.

"Yes." He looked down at our joined hands. "His wife didn't make it. She was already dead when he arrived at the hospice."

"Wow. That sucks," said CJ, with her usual flippancy, and I gave her a hard look.

The man had betrayed the organisation he'd dedicated his whole life to, and plunged mankind into a new age of torment, all to save the wife he adored. And his precious gift of healing had arrived too late to make that terrible price worthwhile. I wondered if the Morrigan had known, even as she gave it to him, how worthless her gift was. Bet she did.

Instead of fleeing, or wallowing in his grief, he'd come back to use that hard-won gift for some kind of good. That must have taken balls. I had to give him that.

"What happened to the Morrigan?" I asked. How come there'd been anyone left for him to save? The Morrigan wasn't exactly the forgiving type. I would have expected her to wreak vengeance on the spot for the destruction of the cauldron.

"The Morrigan and the king and queen took the full brunt of the blast when the cauldron exploded." Dad's face showed a certain grim satisfaction. "They fled back to Tir na nÓg to recover."

"Do you think they'll die?" CJ asked.

Dad snorted. "We should be so lucky. No, they'll heal up well enough. The Sidhe are notoriously hard to kill. I'm sure we'll be seeing them again, and probably sooner than we'd like."

There was a quiet knock, and someone cracked the door open just enough to peek inside. From my angle I couldn't see who it was, but Dad smiled.

"But here's someone I'm sure you'll be pleased to see again." He gestured at the peeker to come in, and the door swung open to reveal Sona's grinning face.

"Vi!" She bounded across the room and threw herself on me. "You're awake. Finally! I thought you were going to sleep the whole day away."

"I had a big night." I hugged her hard. It was so good to see her back to normal. "But look at you! You look amazing. How did you—"

"Dorian," she said. "He used his magic fingers on me. Oh, wait. That sounds wrong."

I laughed. She didn't seem any worse for wear after her ordeal.

"What about Sergei?" I hardly dared hope, but the Morrigan had said Dorian's superpowered healing abilities would last until the next moonrise.

Dad nodded. "Dorian met him at the airport as soon as his flight landed this morning. He's back to normal, and so happy about it I don't think all the rest of it has sunk in yet. I'm not sure he even realises that Dorian caused the whole thing."

"How did he do it?" I asked. "Do you know?"

"When Rebecca first became sick last year, he took a mirror from the vault and charged it with aether."

"My mirror?" CJ asked.

"No. We have several locked away. He used it to contact the Sidhe and bargain with them for Rebecca's life. Their price, of course, was that he had to help them escape. So he started the first leaks and let Puck free to begin his mischief."

"Why didn't he just let them all out straight away?"

"Because it's not that easy to dismantle a prison like the Gilded Cage. It was built by many people working together, and required the power of all four treasures of the Sidhe. Destroying it would take nearly as much effort, and the four treasures had to be present again."

"That was why he was so keen to have another anchoring ceremony," I said. I'd already worked that much out for myself. "So he had an excuse to get all the treasures back together again."

"That doesn't make sense," Sona objected. "Why did the Sidhe take the cauldron back to their own land then, if they knew it was needed here to break them out of prison?"

"It was all part of the plan," Dad said. "They had to make us believe they were on the point of breaking free. We had to be afraid enough so that Dorian could talk the rest of the warders into the re-anchoring. So they started their fear campaign with the fairytale curses, targeting warders and their families. Puck even went for a jaunt down College Street and allowed himself to be captured there, to make us think the Sidhe were after the treasures. A fear that was only confirmed by the Morrigan stealing the cauldron away."

"And then they made it easy for us to steal it back," CJ said slowly. "That was why Ariel contacted me, and helped us get into fairyland. They *wanted* us to take the cauldron."

"It wasn't *that* easy," I objected. "They managed to trap you."

"That was probably a spur of the moment thing," Dad said. "The Sidhe can't resist the opportunity to cause mischief." He smiled. "I bet they're regretting it now."

Yes. Losing the great cauldron of the Dagda wouldn't have been part of their plans.

"What will happen to Dorian now?" CJ asked.

"Well, obviously he can't be a warder any more." He sighed. "Not that any of us can, since there's nothing left to ward."

"But you can't let the Sidhe run wild. Can't you build a new prison?"

He shook his head. "I think the Sidhe are like toothpaste. Once it's out of the tube, there's no putting it back in."

"But you'll still fight them, won't you?"

"If we can. We'll have to think of a new name."

"What about Sidhe-busters?" said Sona.

"I was thinking something a little more upmarket," he said drily.

CJ was still hung up on the question of Dorian. "But what about Dorian?"

"What about him?"

"Well, aren't you going to punish him? You can't just let him get away with it. He's destroyed a two hundred-year-old prison and set a race of magical predators loose on the world. You're always telling us that actions have consequences."

Dad sighed. "I understand that you're angry with him. We've all been through a lot because of his actions. Believe me, I'm angry too. But he's not all bad."

"You mean because he came back to help last night?" I asked.

"That, and the fact that he really didn't want to do it. He just felt he had no choice. For a while there it looked like Rebecca had beaten the cancer, and he broke off communications with the Sidhe."

"Is that why the fairytale attacks stopped after you became a bear?" That made sense. Mum had said Rebecca's cancer was back only a couple of weeks ago, and the next thing we knew Sona had been cursed with the red shoes. Plan A must have been back on the minute Dorian realised that Rebecca was running out of time. No wonder he'd looked so awful. Bad enough to know that your wife was dying, without having to destroy your whole life's work as well.

"That's right. He thought he could forget the whole thing." He sighed. "Sadly, that wasn't to be. But you know, CJ, I don't think we could devise any punishment that could be greater than what he's already going through with the loss of Rebecca. I know how I'd feel if I lost your mum."

"Where *is* Mum?" I asked. I could hardly wait to see my whole family back together. It was like a dream come true. If only Zac was here too it would be perfect. No one else could fill that Zac-sized hole in my heart.

He smiled at me. "She was in here earlier checking on you. I sent her to get some sleep. She had a big night too, and a long flight."

"What about you? Aren't you tired?"

He laughed. "I think I slept so much as a bear that I won't need to sleep again for another month at least. I feel great."

"Yeah. Me too. We don't have to stay in bed any more, do we?"

"No, of course not. I'll go tell the others you're awake." He leaned forward and dropped a kiss on my forehead. CJ got one too, and then he went out and closed the door behind him.

The three of us looked at each other. There was so much to say, and at the same time, no need to say anything.

Sona's tummy rumbled loudly, breaking the silence.

"Well, I don't know about you guys, but I'm ready for breakfast. I haven't eaten in ages! See you in the kitchen?"

"Yep."

We waved her off, and CJ stretched luxuriously. "You coming?"

"Guess so." Everything suddenly seemed so normal again—and yet, everything had changed. "I wonder what's happening out there."

"With the Sidhe?" When I nodded she shrugged. "Before you woke up Dad was saying there'd been quite a few reports on the news. Strange things happening last night. Weird characters. A couple of mysterious deaths. I guess they're enjoying their freedom."

She got up and grabbed a pair of denim shorts and a rather crumpled T-shirt from the floor and got dressed. A used tissue fell from the pocket of the shorts, but she ignored it. It blended in with the rest of her mess on the carpet anyway.

"Don't be long," she said from the doorway, "or I'll eat all the pancakes."

I took my time getting up, enjoying the calm after the stresses of the last few weeks. I knew it was only a temporary reprieve. Things would get exciting soon enough, in new and probably alarming ways. What chance did the battered warders have against the Sidhe now that they were free and determined to make up for lost time?

Sure, there was plenty of aether in the world again, more than enough to power a hundred times the tools and gadgets they had at their disposal. Some of those might even work against the lesser Sidhe, who didn't look too dangerous anyway. I couldn't imagine Dewdrop ever hurting anyone, for instance. But the king and queen and all those haughty types prancing about on their horses? They were bad news. Not to mention the Morrigan, who was going to be royally pissed and looking for someone to take it out on once she recovered. We were going to need a lot more to have a hope of saving anyone from them. Would Zac still be safe? Was England far enough away from her vengeance?

I scratched absently at my arm. There was a tickling, tingling sensation there, as if I'd slept on it funny. Had been ever since I'd woken up, though I'd been too distracted by the others to pay much attention. Now it was starting to bother me, and the other arm was almost as bad.

My gaze fell on the crumpled dirty tissue CJ had dropped in the middle of the floor, and I sighed. I loved my sister with all my heart, but God! Did she have to be such a pig? I glared at that tissue as if it were personally responsible for the evils of the world, and wished it a thousand miles from here.

And, just like that, it vanished.

THE END

Thank you for reading! If you enjoyed *The Cauldron's Gift*, please take a moment to leave a short review where you bought it. Your feedback helps other readers find the book, and I would be very grateful for your assistance in helping to spread the word.

Don't miss the next book, coming soon! For news on this, plus special deals and other book news, sign up for my newsletter.

Sign up by visiting my website, www.marinafinlayson.com.

Also by Marina Finlayson

MAGIC'S RETURN SERIES

The Fairytale Curse

The Cauldron's Gift

THE PROVING SERIES

Moonborn

Twiceborn

The Twiceborn Queen

Twiceborn Endgame

Acknowledgements

Thanks once again to my resident beta readers, Mal, Jen and Alana, for your help with catching my oopses and your general support.

About that dedication: Brian Caswell is now a highly regarded writer of Young Adult fiction, but when I knew him he was my Year 8 English teacher. He read several of the stories I was working on at the time, including my first completed "novel", which was a melodramatic Georgette Heyer rip-off. Despite probably wanting to laugh at my teenaged efforts, he took me seriously and gave helpful critical feedback. He was the first person apart from my mother to encourage my dream of being a writer.

Teachers really can make a difference in the lives of their students. Thanks, Mr Caswell.

About the Author

Marina Finlayson is a reformed wedding organist who now writes fantasy. She is married and shares her Sydney home with three kids, a large collection of dragon statues and one very stupid dog with a death wish.

Her idea of heaven is lying in the bath with a cup of tea and a good book until she goes wrinkly.

www.ingramcontent.com/pod-product-compliance
Lightning Source LLC
Chambersburg PA
CBHW031239120726
47905CB00002B/650